MISFIT LIL RIDES IN

A band of Apache bucks has forsaken reservation life to go on a bloody rampage. In pursuit with Lieutenant Michael Covington's detail is civilian scout Jackson Farraday, but a showdown looms between the pair. Jackson is misled by Lilian Goodnight, an admiring harum-scarum youngster who boasts the handle Misfit Lil, Princess of Pistoleers. After a clash with the Apaches and the slaughter of an Army paymaster, Jackson is fired, but his troubles are only just beginning. He is also framed for murder by crooked Sheriff 'Wheezer' Skene. Can Misfit Lil make amends by saving her reluctant hero?

MISFIT LIL RIDES IN

MISFIT LIL RIDES IN

by

Chap O'Keefe

Dales Large Print Books
Long Preston, North Yorkshire,
BD23 4ND, England.

British Library Cataloguing in Publication Data.

O'Keefe, Chap
    Misfit Lil rides in.

    A catalogue record of this book is
    available from the British Library

    ISBN   978-1-84262-545-3 pbk

First published in Great Britain in 2006 by Robert Hale Limited

Published in Large Print 2007 by arrangement with
Robert Hale Ltd.

Dales Large Print is an imprint of Library Magna Books Ltd.

Printed and bound in Great Britain by
T.J. (International) Ltd., Cornwall, PL28 8RW

1

WILD CHILD

Trouble brewed in McHendry's saloon at Silver Vein, though it would have taken an informed observer to know it.

Cowpunchers and miners – tough, hardy men, most packing guns – crowded the room, for it was a Saturday night. A haze of tobacco smoke, while diffusing light to no convenience, masked a level of body stink that would have been unbearable in its absence. Serious drinking was under way. Voices droned and sometimes shouted with raucous laughter. Silver dollars tinkled. Stakes in games of chance escalated with every turn and slap of the cards, every click and roll of the dice.

But the real danger lay in one slender figure lounging against the long bar.

'Who's the dude proppin' up the counter, Frank?' asked Cole Lansbury. 'Looks kinda outa place in the fringed buckskin duds, like some lost ol' mountain man, though I figger he's awful young, bein' whisker-free.'

'Skinny, too, don't yuh reckon?' his drinking partner said. Then Frank Randolph sniggered, and lowered his voice to a more confidential tone. 'That ain't no he; that's Lilian Goodnight, daughter of cattle rancher Ben Goodnight.'

Lansbury blinked and peered again through the clouds of fug. The figure at the bar did have a certain suppleness, a curve in its lines. Moreover, the buckskin fringe across its chest was lifted a mite, hinting it could be concealing the small breasts of a bony girl.

'What the hell's she doin' in here?' he said, aggrieved at his deception. 'She sure ain't a saloon gal. Like no lady of the night I ever saw neither.'

'That's on account o' she ain't one, Cole. Nor any kind o' lady,' Randolph said. 'She prefers cowboyin'. It's some story round-about.'

Lansbury grunted. 'Do tell.'

Randolph revealed how, a year back, Ben Goodnight had in vexation sent his harum-scarum girl East to a high-toned boarding-school for education and, he hoped, refinement. Proud as the cattleman father was of Miss Lilian's skills as a horsewoman, her expert roping of calves and driving of cows, it wasn't 'proper' that she should be mixing with the ranch-hands, delighting at out-scoring them in most of their skills. Out-cussing them, too.

Life wasn't easy for a widower raising a girl-child. Increasingly, she reminded him of her late mother's beauty. Also she'd inherited her independent character plus, though Ben might not have admitted it, a dash of several generations of Goodnight males' own spirit of adventure.

He thought of marrying her off, if only to get her off his full hands. But he'd have to pity as much as envy the poor sucker who might fall for her and the trick. Till young Lilian was tamed, it wouldn't hardly be right. She'd give the man hell, unless he was uncommonly strong-willed. The paradox in that was the unlikelihood of a self-deter-mined male allowing his level head to be so turned as to get hitched with his rascal daughter in the first place. Thus the good Mr Goodnight plumped for the salvation of education.

Arriving in Boston, Miss Lilian's style was sorely cramped by the private academy for gentlewomen, her freedom curtailed. A par-ticular deprivation was the excitement and release to be had in strenuous physical exercise, to which she'd grown accustomed in the outdoors of the West.

She sought compensation in activity of the only breathtaking sort available within her new confines. This was in the company of the exclusive academy's handsome, eighteen-year-old gardener's-boy. Soon, her classmates – enlightened in the dormitory after lights-out by her whispered extra-curriculum teaching of certain generally suppressed facts – were practically lining up outside the shed in the dark tree shadows at the end of the establishment's walled gardens. They were keen to taste for themselves the sweets of abandon. The gardener's-boy, though not exceptionally bright, was healthily endowed and an enthusiastic recruit to the blushing but curious young ladies' further education.

Initial sacrifice in the cause of keeping their peers' respect and attaining the promised pleasure brought some the inevitable discomfort.

'But shucks, once they were over that pertic'lar, them spoilt rich gals got hell-bent on wearin' their willin' feller clean down to a candle-end,' Randolph said.

Their sampling of forbidden delights, and the giggling, secretive comparing of their thrilling experiences, were not long kept hidden from the eagle-eyed old maids who ran the academy.

Shame! Scandal! The young women's downfall was seen as irregular, irrevocable and hugely damaging. An inquisition by a testy board of governors and the 'seductress' was packed off on a train back West to her despairing father. Another unfortunate pupil was incarcerated in an insane asylum, the Massachusetts State Lunatic Hospital at Taunton, suffering 'venereal feelings from excitement'. Yet the gardener's-boy, it was rumoured, became the very personal companion of the headmistress, and was installed in a rented cottage nearby. Since the headmistress was reputed to be as ugly and old as any sin she railed against, his fate was judged no more desirable.

Of course, the story of Lilian Goodnight's unseemly conduct travelled the same route as the disgraced young lady, maybe not by rail, maybe even faster. Such even then was the transcontinental celerity of a juicy bit of gossip, particularly if it had to do with wantonness among the rich, young and beautiful.

'Miss Lilian' became 'Misfit Lilian' in recognition of her failure to fit in with the affronted academy's strait-laced ways and her resulting expulsion. But effective nick-names are seldom allowed more syllables than what has preceded them. Eventually the cut-down handle 'Misfit Lil' was adopted by most everyone.

'Why then,' Cole Lansbury opined, 'she ain't no better than a dirty little whore.'

'Shh!' Frank Randolph warned. 'Don't let Lil hear yuh say that, or she might challenge yuh to a gun-duel.'

'Take more'n a gal to best me,' came the retort, more in disbelief than as a brag. His right hand dropped reflexively to hover over the butt of his Colt.

'Don't count on it, Cole. She's a better crackshot than any of her pa's 'punchers. I seen her use the six-gun she totes on that thar lean hip. She'll make a tin can dance along Main Street no trouble. And once she hammered five four-inch nails halfways into a boardwalk post, then drove each of 'em in with a bullet from twenty paces.'

'Yuh're joshin' me!'

'Nope. The post split an' the damn' awnin' fell right down. Sheriff Skene slapped Misfit Lil in the hoosegow. She had to stay locked up till her pa came inta town next day an' paid the damages. He grumbled somethin' fierce about havin' to put up with his wild child's foolishness.'

Cole Lansbury stared at Misfit Lil's back trying to picture her wielding a blazing Colt. The picture, once summoned, riled him. A girl showing off with a gun! Moreover, he didn't like it that he'd been fooled in front of Frank Randolph into thinking she was a man. And worse, he didn't like it when she wigwagged her slender fingers in the recognized manner and the barkeep dutifully delivered a bottle from the top shelf. This was private stock; no cheap redeye. The label declared Very Old Scotch Whisky.

'The bitch...' he said under his foul breath.

She took a glass of the strong drink straight down and poured a second before she seemed to sense his glowering stare. She took a well-worn riding boot off the brass rail at the foot of the bar-front and turned. Once she'd stopped leaning on the bar, she looked lithe and fit. She gave him his look back – level, eye to eye.

'You got a problem, mister?' She was direct of gaze and voice. Chilly? Steely? Maybe.

On the instant, Lansbury should have been informed she was better than any Western man had a right to expect, and knew it. But a puritanical streak in his make-up wouldn't let him rid his mind of the shocking image of a Boston lad, naked and hugely aroused, and he resented her straightforward way, her guileless face. Pride and the liquor he'd been taking on board over the past hour did the rest for him.

'Yeah... I don't like no filthy female shams clutterin' up a man's waterin'-hole,' he blustered on. 'Why don't yuh move on out, lady?'

A flash of anticipatory animation crossed Misfit Lil's features at the last word, as though a gauntlet had been thrown down. But she shrugged and indicated her near-full bottle.

'I've business here. It's a hell of a ride from the Flying G for less'n a quarter of a pint.' She was still grave, but the voice now held a softly amused tone and the edge of a smile tugged at the corners of her not unpretty mouth.

To Lansbury this signified nothing despite the cautionary tale of her skills his sidekick had told. He got short and presumptuous.

'Vamoose, girlie!'

'I don't want to argue with you, mister, but what if I don't?' She spoke with remarkable soberness considering the bottle was not her first order of the night. But on

14

Lansbury's reckoning, she had to be drunk rather than just comfortable.

'I'll *make yuh* is what!'

'Oh? And how? D'you think you're going to kick my ass or something?'

The developing altercation had come to the notice of the wider company. A hush of interest fell. Maybe of expectation. A wag in the furthest, weakest-lit corner of the room daringly piped up, 'Naw ... he can do better things with a man-teasin' tail like your'n!'

The ripple of mocking laughter this provoked pushed Lansbury over the edge. Red-faced, he went for his gun. It was the worst thing he could have done, and he paid the price for his folly.

A searing pain went through his forearm to the accompaniment of an explosive roar. His hand from the wrist down was stricken totally numb. Even so, last reflexes squeezed the trigger of his cocked and raised weapon before it clattered to the floor.

The scene burned itself into Lansbury's brain in a slow-motion tableau that would return to haunt his nightmares long after. Immediately before him was a rapidly clearing path across the sawdust to Misfit Lil. The girl's six-gun was in her fist, smoking. Behind her was the counter, beyond that the big back-bar mirror and scores of ranked bottles – the whole collapsing into a thousand crashing shards since Lansbury's own shot had wildly and widely missed its mark.

Patrons yelled and kicked over tables; dropped behind them. Who knew what would follow the first round of gunfire?

McHendry himself, gone white and trembling with fearful rage, hauled out his shotgun from under the counter, the last resort in moments of frontier-bar crisis.

He never got to speak.

The deafening roar of the two close shots still had ears ringing, and the reeking, coiling powdersmoke was barely beginning to stratify and spread over the assembly, augmenting the rich tobacco clouds, when...

Outside, a growing clatter of hoofs hammered to a stop at the hitch rail. Oblivious of the tense situation within, an agitated newcomer thrust through the batwings at a run, unaware he was breaking an abrupt near-silence. He sped across the bullet-cleared space to the bar, slapped his hands on it and dropped his head, panting.

'Gimme a shot, quick!'

The urgency of the arrival's demand had the barkeep automatically slopping spirit from an intact bottle into a waiting glass while a hubbub of questions was thrown at him by the ready audience.

'What in blue blazes, Riocca...?'

'Tell us the news, Luke!'

'Who's chasin' yuh?'

Many missed Luke Riocca's throaty answer in the noise of their own shouted enquiries.

'A bunch of crazy-wild, renegade 'Paches has jumped the reservation! Killing, looting – burned off least two spreads north ... Parker's, Olsen's.'

The pandemonium swelled as those who'd heard conveyed the information to those who hadn't. Heated conjecture escalated word of the raids to a whole new Indian war.

Cole Lansbury, the courage running out of him with the blood that dripped from his arm, slumped into a chair. He moaned involuntarily with pain.

'Jesus, Frank ... the crazy bitch's hurt my arm real awful.' He began tying a bandanna around his arm above the wound.

Randolph tutted. 'It could as soon've been between your eyes, pard, if she'd a mind. Ain't for nothin' she bin called Princess o' Pistoleers. Guess she didn't want the heap o' trouble.'

Nobody else noticed Lansbury's predicament.

17

Misfit Lil... Well, nobody noticed what she did either. Not even the unhappy McHendry who'd entertained passing thoughts of coercing her wealthy father into paying for the breakage of his expensive mirror. It was many minutes before the uproar subsided and the freshly agitated crowd stopped milling. By then the unconventional young woman was long and quietly gone, slipping into the falling night.

Misfit Lil regretted the incident at Mc-Hendry's. More than that, its sudden closure was less than satisfying, and it would again be advisable for her to steer clear of the Flying G and her long-suffering father.

She rode her obedient pinto cow pony along a winding, rising trail out of the Silver Vein township. There was no moon and eventually timber closed around them. She was then under a shroud of dense blackness, broken raggedly here and there where the trail widened so that through the bordering trees she could glimpse a star-dotted sky.

Damp night smells of piñon and other growth rose around her, particularly in the dips. Far off, a coyote howled. She heard all the little sounds closer about just as well, and knew what they were.

A frown came to her clean features.

How was she to occupy herself now? The Indian trouble sounded frightening, but exciting. The army was after the renegades, Luke Riocca had said. A detachment of cavalry led by stuck-up Lieutenant Michael Covington, all spruce and dashing and enough to set most girls' hearts aflutter (though *never* hers), was allegedly in hot pursuit from Fort Dennis. The soldiers also had Jackson Farraday, the scout and guide, along with them.

She sighed. Now Farraday was the genuine article, and a real man ... except he was twice her age and always failed to give her a second look.

Maybe she'd track the cavalry and offer her additional services. She knew the country inside out. One day, she might make a top scout herself, if only the likes of Covington and Farraday would give her some recognition. Finding their party held a promise of new fun, too.

Meantime, though she hadn't much in way of supplies, she was armed and ready for anything in the line of rugged mischief. And hadn't she brought along her interrupted bottle?

2

DESERT DANGER

Under a brassy sky, the small detachment of cavalry slogged further into the high desert country, its dusty, lather-crusted horses dangerously close to exhaustion.

The civilian scout Jackson Farraday reflected grimly that whatever forces had created this desolate landscape had no love of humankind. It was a place of treachery and slow death for all but the wary and knowledgeable.

The charismatic Apache hothead Angry-he-shakes-fist was among the knowing ones. His marauding band of young bucks, after forsaking reservation life, had preyed swiftly on the white man's horse and cattle herds, torching isolated settlements and raiding a freighter's mule train. They'd picked up food, horses and a lot of ammunition. But then they'd climbed from the productive flatlands into the badlands.

Farraday recognized the tactic well enough.

The vastness of sun-scorched rock around him, all reddish brown and ochre, was riven with a maze of winding canyons that provided natural escape routes, though sign was almost invisible that man ever set foot here. Angry-fist knew the lore of his ancestors and might find the few springs and seep-holes along the way to succour his parched band and their tough, wiry mustangs. Meanwhile, the bluecoats, led astray into dry back canyons where no water was to be found, would become disorientated, lose their way and die of starvation or dehydration.

The troop topped out on a plateau. Spread before them was a savage land of violently configured steeples and peaks, buttes and mesas, with deep gullies and gulches dividing them. If any of this mass of rocky formations was the product of an intelligence, it could only be a warped, twisted one. It was the Devil's own country.

Lieutenant Michael Covington was losing his patience with Jackson's plodding pursuit of the renegades, looking for the scraped rock, the turned pebble. He prided himself on immaculate appearance. Neither he, nor the men of his detail, nor their mounts could lay any claim to that. They were bone-tired, drooping and stained with sweat.

'This will put us in a bad light, Mr Farraday,' the flushed lieutenant said. 'Angry-fist has gotten clean away. I'm sickened of traipsing across this wilderness. You've let him trick us on to some wild goose chase for sure.'

'I hope not,' Jackson murmured. 'He's just a young Apache delinquent leading us white-eyes a dance across some mountains is all.'

For all that he had no fine uniform, he was the one of the company who'd preserved the most dignity. He was a stern, quietly spoken man in his late thirties, tall in the saddle and broad-shouldered, wearing a much-washed and well-worn green shirt and broadcloth pants tucked into thigh length boots. A wide-brimmed felt hat shaded a weather-burnished face from which pale, blue-grey eyes stared out to take calm stock above a fairly trim chin-beard and moustache. His hair was long, falling to his shoulders, and bleached near-white by the blazing sun under which he'd spent so many of his days.

Like most of the army's civilian scouts, Jackson was hired by the month or for specific expeditions. In the past, he'd supplied buffalo meat for railroad construction outfits and carried dispatches through hostile

Indian territory. He understood the natives' situation better than many of his peers, and didn't always see eye to eye with the military, like now when he was dealing with a less experienced, younger man too inclined to lean on his West Point training.

Covington bristled as he was contradicted.

'Apache murderer if we leave him the chance! He has to be hunted own. Harsh reprisals should be taken against every member of his clan of savages.'

A dumpy trooper with cropped flaxen hair tried to maintain the fracturing peace. 'Beggin' pardon, sirs, Angry-fist's horses can't be in no better shape than our own, though that were a nice string of mares he stole offa the Parker place afore he set the barns afire.'

'Angry-fist ain't riding those horses,' Jackson said, with a shake of his head and tight grin. 'If he still has them, he's only taking them along till they drop. He has his hardy little mustangs. The mares mean nothing to him other than possible meat on the hoof.'

Covington reasserted his authority. 'Well, I've had a gutful of fruitless casting-about over acres of sun-blasted rock. I insist you lead us back to the timber-line, Mr Farraday, then forthwith to the flats and the stage road to Fort Dennis.'

'Why for, Lieutenant? We want to find Angry-fist's raiding party, don't we? And my instincts tell me we're not alone up here. I've gotten a gut feeling about it. We've been shadowed all day.'

Covington half-sneered. 'Is that so, Mr Farraday? You believe Angry-fist is playing games with us, is that it?'

'Someone is.'

'I don't believe it.' He turned in his saddle, pointedly surveying the boulders strewn around them as though Jackson had claimed an Apache was about to jump up from behind every one of them. 'Imagination!'

Jackson rose to no bait. 'Why do you think we should be on the stage road?' he asked.

'Because Angry-fist might have gotten wind of the army paymaster's wagon. It makes a regular journey, and it arrives at Fort Dennis tomorrow.'

'Fiddlesticks,' Jackson said dismissively, but without enmity. 'The red man has no interest in the white man's pay. Largely, it's his livestock, trinkets and whiskey that might grab his thoughts – the beads and the mirrors and the blankets. The guns.'

'He'll get none of those,' Covington said with a determined lift of a square-cut chin darkened, to his chagrin, with two days' growth of stubble.

Jackson mused, 'Doesn't the paymaster have his own escort?'

'Of course, but there'll be no harm in having reinforcements on hand, and we're doing no good out here. If Angry-fist were to show, which I greatly doubt, our horses would be too tired to put to the chase.'

On that they could agree.

Reluctantly, Jackson led the cavalry back across the blistering rocks, skirting plunging ravines and passing through sheer-walled canyons. He was still of the opinion that after a night's appropriate rest they should return to combing the badlands.

The notion that they were followed every halting step of the way stayed with him. He was uneasy, fearing an ambush. It was hellish country, made for the possibility. The more broken the landscape, the stronger was his sixth sense of being observed.

Jackson Farraday had held quite a reputation for this sensitivity during campaigns against the Indians in south-eastern Arizona and south-western New Mexico. He'd brushed with the forces led by the One-who-yawns, or Geronimo to give him the Spanish name by which he was known to the world.

With this memory, the thought occurred to him that the unseen watcher was one alone, not a band. He might be using field glasses at a distance. He rode on with apparent unconcern, but he cast his searching gaze around and extended its range to take in highest and furthest crags and outcrops. No betraying glint of sun on glass rewarded him. He grunted to himself.

The watcher was careful.

At the jaws of a canyon, Jackson hesitated. In the dust underfoot were many hoofprints, the marks of their own outward-bound journey, now being matched print for print by their return.

He frowned. At more than one point, could he not make out a strange set of impressions going uphill which wasn't duplicated in the reverse?

It confirmed his suspicions, but he said nothing.

They regained slopes peppered with junipers and sagebrush, and then travelled through a pass which led them downgrade to the merciful shade of taller timber late in the afternoon. Further west, the great yellow-grass flatlands of the basin spread out before them below a sinking amber sun that seemed benevolent after the furnace heat of the higher, barren country.

The rough trail widened into a meadow, bounded on one side by the piñon and on the other by an up-and-down canyon wall of red rock, hundreds of feet high. At its base was a trickle of a creek which at one point had formed a small but useful pool. The available water and the grass made it a welcome campsite for the night.

'We'll have to camp someplace,' Jackson said. 'Travel at night in this country is ill-advised. Just because we haven't seen any Apaches don't mean there aren't any, or haven't been any.'

Covington agreed but with an abruptness that suggested the decision was forced on him.

'We'll stay here until light.'

At sundown, the still air was tempered by a balmy wind from the high mountains that created an illusion of chill. It felt good on burned skin and eased aching limbs. A camp-fire was built; coffee brewed. Some bacon was found and cooked, adding to the comforting aroma.

Covington briskly posted sentries. How like him, Jackson thought. It would be army regulations, Article 1a, Section 2b, Paragraph 3c. Or somesuch. But he was glad of it and would have recommended the precaution himself. Chances were hostile Indians were in the vicinity somewhere, and he still had the unnerving sense of being under observation.

The first confirmation they were not alone was a rattle of sliding shale in amongst the brush.

The suddenness and closeness of the ominous sound made skin crawl. The soldiers, shapes sat backed vulnerably against the firelight, forgot the mugs of coffee in their hands and exchanged alarmed glances.

Jackson, sitting slightly apart, was on his feet instantly. His right hand drew the Frontier Colt which had its seven and a half inches nestled in a smooth-worn, saddle-soaped holster against his thigh.

'Come on out of it!' he snapped into the darkness.

Getting past Michael Covington's fatigued sentries was child's play to Lilian Good-night. But the one false step on the shale was not part of her plan. 'Must be losing my touch,' she muttered in self-disgust.

No help for it when Jackson Farraday made his challenge. She called out, 'Easy, fellers,

I'm coming in with both hands empty!'

She emerged from the jumble of rocks and undergrowth to immediate recognition. Misfit Lil was a figure of some small notoriety in the territory that took in Fort Dennis, the reservation, the Boorman's Wells trading post, the mining and ranching township of Silver Vein, and the basin where the biggest spread was the Flying G.

'Miss Goodnight!' Covington exclaimed. 'What in heaven's name are you doing up here?'

'Right now, Mike, I'd be a-begging for a mug of that heady-smelling coffee your men are brewing.'

Covington straightened his back and drew himself up.

'The name is Lieutenant Covington, miss. Your familiarity before enlisted men shows a lack of appropriate decorum, while your very presence in the wilderness without escort and at a dangerous time is an unwanted imposition.'

'Pshaw! I was born and raised in these parts. These are my canyons and mountains. I know this land like eastern kids know their backyards. I know it clear to the Colorado River and covering the Old Spanish Trail to Circleville in one direction

29

and Santa Fe the other.'

She could have said she knew most every gully and cave, every abandoned shack and soddy, the short-cuts, the detours to each point of the compass. She knew them like a sea pilot would know the currents and rips, the small islands and hidden rocks – the treacherous shallows – that made navigation of his native coastline hazardous to those who didn't share its secrets.

'But what of the hostiles, young lady?' Covington asked as though he was scoring a point.

Misfit Lil put on her own airs. 'Not so much of the *young lady*, Mike. I'm almost as old as yourself in years, and in some kinds of experience I'm older, I reckon.'

Titters from unidentifiable troopers made Covington's face redden. 'The *hostiles*, I say!' he persisted.

'Yeah, what of 'em? No call to blow your cork. Can't I out-ride and out-shoot any of those Apache kids?'

Jackson horned in on the verbal tussle. 'Miss Lilian, you might not be one, but to some here you're just a chit of a pesky gal. All day I knew someone was lurking around us, and to speak plain it was a nuisance. Why don't you just ride in your mount, set yourself down and have some of the coffee you've a hankering for?'

'Obliged,' she said stiffly. 'I'll go walk my horse in.'

She left, happy to vanish momentarily from the men's sight. She was cut by Jackson's words in a way she wasn't by Covington's. Mike was a bit of a fool to her way of thinking. But Jackson was something else. She wanted his approval more than she wanted any other thing that was in her world. She wanted the incidental nod of equality from the skilled, tough scout who had ridden far trails and held his own among people of all kinds. For, although she would never publicly admit it, she was a hero-worshipper and her pattern was Jackson Farraday. Too bad he was so *old...*

She made her second entrance to the camp leading a weary horse, which she took to where the soldiers had picketed theirs by the stream. She unsaddled and saw to her animal. The voices of Jackson Farraday and Mike Covington came murmuring over to her. Seemingly unaware she could hear them, they were talking about her.

'She must've been in the offing, stalking us. I knew someone was there,' Jackson said.

'Like a savage Indian prowler, Mr Farraday. White men don't prowl.'

'Were she an Injun, we might know better what to do with her.'

Covington digested this. 'Well, of course. Then it would be much easier. But she's a white girl, damnit. The West is no place for anyone' – he waved an arm to encompass the greater inhospitable area – 'the wind, the dust, the bleakness – let alone for a civilized woman fooling about. What if she'd fallen into the hands of Angry-fist's bunch of bloodthirsty Apaches?'

'We would've had to pray,' was Jackson's level rejoinder.

'To *pray?*' Covington was scoffing.

Jackson chuckled. 'For the Indians, of course.'

Coming back toward the gathering, but keeping herself outside the fireglow, Lil had difficulty restraining her indignation.

'Balderdash!' Covington said. 'The girl's biting off more than she can chew this time, despite her reputation. How did she find us, anyway?'

'Like she said, she was born and raised in this country. These are her mountainsides. She has an instinct for tracking and her skills are second to many experienced men's I've known.'

At these words, Lil's consternation dissipated as quickly as it had formed. She savoured the scout's praise.

'You could send her away, of course,' Jackson went on.

Covington's chin lifted. 'I think not, Mr Farraday. My duty is crystal-clear: to return her to her home, which is the place for all respectable women.'

'Duty is a cheerless master, Lieutenant.'

'I'll endure her accompanying us only because I have to,' came the more brittle reply. 'She is an impossible creature.'

Jackson shrugged. 'Well, sure, Misfit Lil's no better than she should be, but someday she'll be a good companion for some true Western man. If she was more my own age, I would never let the talk stop me: I'd accept her as she was.'

It dawned on Covington that Jackson saw Lil as maybe a little more than fit company.

'Are you suggesting I should *pay court* to this female?' he said, gasping in outrage. 'You must be blind, man! Even the mannish clothes she wears are an impropriety.'

Lil could contain herself no longer. She stormed into plain view and confronted Covington, arms akimbo.

'Dumb beeves don't mind these duds,

Mike Covington! Why should you?'

Covington recovered quickly from his surprise at Lil's sudden entrance into what he'd supposed had been a private conversation. He smiled thinly.

'They might look all right to a cow, I'll allow,' he said. 'But gentlemen like something that brings out the grace in a woman, you know.'

'I don't give two hoots and a holler for graces, bluecoat,' she said, her face tightening. 'And I can tell you, your genteel gals don't give a hang for 'em either, once they get with a man under a blanket.'

Covington grated, 'That'll be enough sass, Miss Goodnight! You'll talk with decency.'

Every time she'd run into Mike Covington, the passing encounters had brought friction. The correct and handsome young cavalry officer might impress her peers, but he surely left her cold! No two ways about it, they rubbed each other up the wrong way. He regarded her with contempt. She knew he had to be an idiot from his superbly profiled but pig head to his highly polished boots.

Jackson growled. 'Ease off, you two. If we're in camp together, it's plumb stupid being at each other's throats. Why not taste some of that coffee you were asking for, Miss Lilian?'

Acting peacemaker, he led the trio to the campfire, lifted the coffee pot and poured.

Lil took the offered mug and a long swallow from it. The coffee was as good as its aroma. She smacked her lips with relish.

'Aaah! Thank you, gents. How many years was it at West Point, Mike...? Four? They sure teach soldiers there how to make good coffee.'

Her banter was not appreciated. The lieutenant didn't quite shake with uncontrollable rage, but he was plainly put out. He threw her what she supposed was meant to be a look of withering disgust.

Well, too bad. It was his problem if he didn't have a sense of humour.

3

THE PAYMASTER'S WAGON

Come first light, Covington's detail was ready to break camp and move out. At true dawn in this wilderness the sun climbed swiftly above the jagged horizon and produced instant new heat to burn the skin and blind whatever crazed eyes dared to stare into its cruel intensity.

Jackson Farraday saddled up his rested sorrel mare and rode out from the comparative comfort of the upland meadow with the bluecoats and Lilian Goodnight. The cavalcade moved under the vivid sky at a brisk pace set by their young commander.

'I mean us to travel fast today, Mr Farraday,' the lieutenant told the scout. 'It might be a profitable business for you civilians, this providing tracking services to the army, but on this expedition I can't see that much more has been achieved than sport for an interfering girl. Meanwhile, an army payroll might be in danger while a bunch of renegades runs loose – damn their stinking red hides!'

Jackson understood that Covington was still furious, especially at how he'd ostensibly been fooled by Misfit Lil. But he shrugged philosophically and made no mention of her.

'Weren't no better could be done. Angry-fist passed this way for sure, thinking to fox pursuit. As for the army money, like I said, I can't see what use his bunch would have for it. The paymaster's wagon is safe enough, I reckon.'

Thus it was doubly galling when he eventually had to eat his words.

'Sar! What the blazes is happenin' down thar?'

A soldier raised a cry and pointed to something he'd spotted close to the stage trail winding in from the north across the plains below them. Jackson followed the direction of his out-thrust finger.

He saw a rolling dust ball at a distance of several miles. It was coming pell-mell toward them and growing in size and clarity by the second. Behind it came a score of smaller dust clouds that resolved themselves into a string of savage riders on fleet ponies, racing along behind the larger object.

'My God! It's the pay wagon,' someone

else said in a shocked voice.

Jackson identified the hurtling conveyance as a blue-sided Dougherty wagon. These large, comparatively comfortable carriages were often used by the army as ambulances. Jackson had seen this one before and knew it was assigned for the paymaster's use. It had a large body with two seats facing each other and a seat outside for the driver. The interior could be completely closed by canvas sides and back which rolled up and down, and by a curtain which dropped behind the driver's seat, allowing a degree of privacy. It was drawn by a team of six mules – army beasts which were sleek, well-fed, and trained to trot as fast as the average carriage-horse.

And these mules were moving faster than that now. They were bolting, while the driver, swaying on his seat, looked to be dead. The ribbons were slack in his hands.

'Bugler!' Covington roared. 'Sound the charge! *Forward!*'

The column broke, wheeled and reformed into a line that raced down to intercept the pursuing band of Indians. The fast-moving line broke and diverted only when it was necessary to dodge boulders and the odd scrub oak that dotted the barren slopes.

The wagon on which the Apaches and the soldiers converged was off the road and rocking wildly. The frenzied mules had no chance of outrunning the swift, near-naked, painted and bronze-skinned devils who rushed along in their rear. Several feathered arrows jutted from the sides of the wagon.

In a matter of seconds the Apaches saw or sensed the cavalry descending upon them. With high-pitched yells, the fierce-looking young braves pulled round their ponies to confront the threat to their chase.

Jackson recognized their leader: Angry-fist, sure enough, his painted face set in a wicked grin. A wide headband encircled the straight black hair that streamed out behind him. One large eagle feather jutted up from the headband.

The advancing mounted parties exchanged preliminary shots. They all seemed to miss, which wasn't remarkable. Many of the Indians, Jackson observed, had old and probably stolen carbines, though a handful had new, army-issue repeating rifles, which was puzzling and ominous. They seemed unfamiliar with the weapons, or out of ammunition, since few used them.

'Cease your fire!' Jackson roared in the Apache tongue as they came close.

He heard a zing and an arrow sliced through the edge of his hat's brim. Then they were amongst the band, scattering them.

'Let 'em have it, men!' Covington said.

A withering volley of fire poured into the Apaches, sending several tumbling from their mustangs' backs. The hot air quickly thickened with powder fumes, and the war whoops of the charging braves lost their note of defiance.

Jackson glimpsed Lilian Goodnight. She sat her saddle straight and easy, alert and unafraid. The spirit of the girl, light and quick, was apparent in her posture. Her clean-boned face, usually expressive to him of openness and honesty, albeit overlied by a lively mischief, was sober.

He also noted she'd rashly ridden down-slope in the path of the soldiers and was about to be surrounded by Indians, brandishing tomahawks and spiked war clubs.

'God, no,' he gasped. 'The crazy young fool....'

But she calmly raised her six-gun and picked off the two at closest quarters, showing not a flicker of fear or hesitation. Simultaneously, hellish screams told of two other Apaches fallen elsewhere.

What with the smoke, the rising dust and

the heat shimmers, Jackson couldn't keep track of what happened to Misfit Lil after that. Moreover, he was battling to preserve his own life in the mêlée. He threw lead into a mass of surging redskins unbroken by bluecoats ... till his Colt clicked on an empty chamber.

An Apache closed in on him, and slashed with a wide-bladed knife.

Jackson turned in the saddle, bringing up his arm. He felt his sleeve rip and the blade tear flesh. But he seized the brown wrist. Toppling from his saddle, he dragged the Indian down with him. Together, they rolled about in the dust in a life-and-death struggle.

Jackson strove to pin the redman's wrist to the ground, to prevent him plunging the knife into his vitals. But the youth was strong; his greasy, painted skin as slippery as an eel's.

All about, guns were being fired. Suddenly, and to Jackson's relief, the Indian jerked, exhaling a gasp of hot, stinking breath into his face. He'd been hit, purposely or by a stray shot, Jackson didn't know and couldn't pause to consider. He was in a serious position. Shooting continued, visibility was bad, and the milling horses' hoofs fell indiscriminately.

Guns emptied, some of the troopers had

drawn sabres for the hand-to-hand fight.

At that grave moment, Angry-fist gave a bloodcurdling cry. But it proved to be a call for retreat rather than a prolonging of the short but bloody conflict. His band broke off and fled, the fleet-footed Indian ponies soon outpacing the optimistic troopers who pounded after them on tired and lathered horses.

Beyond reach of the cavalry's blades, the savages yelled belligerently but kept on going.

'Sergeant!' Covington barked.

'Yessir!'

'After that wagon! We don't want a wreck. Stop those dumb brutes before they drag the damn thing over or smash a wheel!'

Jackson recognized that the lieutenant was scathing of the mules only out of exasperation. Mules, not horses, were the true empire builders of the American West. They'd hauled most immigrant wagons; transported most military supplies; were prime farm draught animals. The army had relied heavily both on wagon trains pulled by harness mules and on trains of pack mules.

The sergeant and two other troopers set out after the wagon. But from nowhere Misfit Lil was already heading it off and moving in on the mules.

The six harness animals had dark coats and looked to be sound in all aspects and fully fleshed. They were probably four to ten years old; about thirteen and a half hands high.

The girl acted like she'd been accustomed to working with such beasts all her life.

'Whoa, there, Fanny! Whoa, Kate!'

She snatched at the smart harness of the leading right-hand mule, trimmed off with white ivory rings. She hung on till the panicked but well-trained animals were calmed and slowed.

The three soldiers, catching up, added their weight to pulling the team and the bucketing rig to a halt. Jackson wasn't far behind. Covington paused only to confirm that the wagon driver, whose body had fallen from the high seat to the ground, was beyond aid.

'How'd yuh know their names, miss?' asked the sergeant.

'It were just guesswork, General,' Lil told him with a grin. 'The names had to be them ... or Liza. You soldiers always use those for mules.'

Covington, pulling up alongside the group, said curtly, 'For God's sake, girl, this won't do! You had no business to engage with the hostiles, let alone continue endangering your life. I had taken you under the army's protection.'

'Well, there's thanks for you! In point of fact, I kinda thought I was helping...'

Jackson, surveying her equanimity and the dust-stained, dishevelled and flustered condition of Covington's men, agreed silently with her point. Her courage and marksmanship may even have saved soldiers' lives. As it was, he'd counted three fallen bluecoats who hadn't risen.

But it was time for neither jubilation, nor argument, nor counting the dead. Jackson pulled aside the canvas concealing the interior of the Dougherty and climbed in.

Paymaster Major Pelham was slumped on the floor between the seats. He'd been badly hit by bullets and arrows, one of which stuck out from his back. Under him was a pool of his own blood. The pallor of death was already on him and he was barely conscious. His flickering eyes met Jackson's.

'Injuns wiped out the escort,' he murmured. 'Unbelievable. Dead, all dead. Reckon I'm a-going, too. But they didn't get the pay chest.'

'Bring the medical kit!' Covington rapped.

The order was futile. Pelham had made his last, supreme effort; had effectively made his report and fulfilled his responsibilities. This done, he could hold on to life no longer.

It was a bad business, Jackson allowed. He'd discounted an attack on the paymaster's wagon and been proved wrong. Young Covington wouldn't overlook it.

The lieutenant dispatched half his remaining force to locate and bury Major Pelham's lost escort. The rest of the party headed for the nearest settlement, Boorman's Wells, grouped around the wagon with its grisly burden and the saved pay.

'None of this need have happened,' Covington said. 'We wasted time and resources traipsing to and fro across the canyonlands. What a disastrous fiasco! And Angry-fist still loose. I blame you, Mr Farraday. You and that bothersome Goodnight brat.'

Misfit Lil had sharp ears. 'Did I hear my name, Mike?'

Covington winced. 'You did, but I was talking about you, not to you, and the real subject is something else. The Apaches might have had the civilian expert bamboozled, but not me.'

'Don't know 'bout that, Mike. Trouble

45

with renegade Apaches is a body can't depend on 'em for anything. You can never tell where or when they're going to show up. They might strike once in a vicinity, then vanish. Or they might decide to stay around, waiting for other unwary victims. Ain't a way of knowing with the bastards.'

'Mr Farraday is paid to know,' Covington said, though it must have been because he was nettled by the girl, because it appeared in no contractual arrangements.

Jackson was on a short fuse. His badly gashed arm was paining him and unfair criticism founded on the realization of an unlikely eventuality he could do without. Covington was confident he'd cleverly predicted what Angry-fist would target, but really it had to have been nothing but luck.

'I tell you, Injuns can't use such quantities of white man's scrip and coin,' he grated. 'What happened was beyond figuring, Lieutenant.'

Covington scoffed. 'Then how come I figured it?'

'In that case, maybe there's nothing a trained scout can do for you.'

Covington was equally bitter. 'I'm sure I can do without your services, Mr Farraday.'

Jackson knew when he was dismissed.

46

'That's a full and considered conclusion, Lieutenant?'

'It is. I'll hire another guide if I need one.' His tone was formal and his next words made it final. 'You may collect your pay at Fort Dennis.'

Jackson had his pride. 'Don't think I'll bother to take the ride.'

He knew forfeiting job and money would leave him in a bind. His reputation would be blackened, and he'd be embarrassingly out of pocket.

'Jesus,' said Lil, who seemed startled by the rapidity and seriousness of the falling-out. 'You fellers don't fool around when you lock horns, do you?'

4

REFUGE

Boorman's Wells was not the most restorative of places, but for many people it was a refuge for as many different reasons.

For Axel Boorman, it was a refuge from failure in other parts. Sly and self-satisfied as he was, it was chiefly good luck that he'd hit on establishing his log trading post on the unpromising site. The store was now augmented by an adjoining saloon, while a blacksmith's forge, a stable and a half-dozen surrounding ramshackle cabins and barns were rented out to assorted riff-raff and would-be small ranchers. All of the unlovely structures were the property of the settlement's heavily built, cigar-smoking founder. In this small portion of a land without a monarchy, he was King Axel.

Boorman's Wells did good business with travellers too weary to go the extra miles to Silver Vein and who also saw the post as a refuge – from heat, dust and waterlessness.

But most store custom was from reservation Indians who wanted to trade and drink outside the overview of the military at Fort Dennis. To them, it was a refuge from authoritarianism and insult.

Then there were the townsfolk of Silver Vein and the hands from the bigger outfits, the closest of which was Ben Goodnight's Flying G. On occasion, certain of them would prefer to do their more private drinking, or their noisier roistering, away from fellow men and uninhibited by the law as represented by Sheriff Willard 'Wheezer' Skene. Again, the place was a refuge of sorts, though it still fell within the sheriff's bailiwick.

Appropriately, Boorman's Wells became Jackson Farraday's refuge. Lieutenant Covington's detachment patched itself up, filled its canteens, and set out for Fort Dennis with Major Pelham's scarred pay wagon. Jackson stayed.

Boorman's close-set eyes had been beady and greedy when he made his suggestion.

'It ain't much I can offer, Farraday. Tending bar don't pay army rates. It's no decent way of making a living for a professional scout and tracker.'

The store owner drew on his cigar, taking

long about it while he let Jackson ponder his offer.

His wife, Esther, added her blandishments. 'Why, Jackson, we'd be right glad to have you staying on at the Wells. And Axel's offer would give your poor gashed arm a grand chance to heal. It'd knit right properly in no time. I could dress it daily my ownself...'

Jackson had no other opening in prospect. He needed a job and some ready cash, however little, so he accepted. These menial jobs done for men of Boorman's ilk sometimes worked out. As well as lining the pockets of their self-interested promoters, he had known them to lead to introductions and opportunities.

But overhearing the settling of his fate, Lilian Goodnight, who had a propensity for eavesdropping on significant conversations, was appalled.

'What a hateful idea!' she said afterwards. 'Pouring the rotgut in a low dive like Boorman's saloon. I feel real bad about this. It was me who led you and Mike and his men up and down the canyonlands. Mike's a mean galoot, firing the best scout the army's ever had hereabouts, but it might never've happened if I hadn't butted in.'

'Not true, gal. It was Angry-fist who set us all up first off before doubling back. Anyways, bar work ain't a dishonourable calling and what else is to hand?'

It was a question Misfit Lil couldn't answer. Her pa might have work more fitting on the Flying G, but the explanations wouldn't be easy and the father-daughter relationship was presently strained, a not infrequent state of affairs. As she'd say of herself, 'I'm in the doghouse so doggone often, it seems the natural place to be, but better'n no place at all, I guess.'

What she said now picked up darkly on Boorman's wife's professed concerns.

'Nor do I cotton to Mrs Boorman with her "poor gashed arm" stuff. She's a hotsy-totsy no-good. A troublemaker, and a sight too familiar with the menfolks, you should be informed.'

Jackson laughed. 'Esther's familiarity ain't as forward as it sounded. I knew her way-back-when in Denver. We were just friends, but I'm no stranger to what she is and was.'

'Way-back-when, huh? Like when Adam was a boy and Eve weren't around?'

'Not that far.'

'Hmm! Then I reckon you need to worry. Says in the Bible, "It is not good that the man should be alone." But I ain't always sure about that.'

In truth, Jackson knew a deal more than Misfit Lil about Axel Boorman's woman. North-east, in the booming Colorado city, Esther Peters had at one time been an unsuccessful faro dealer, but also a well-patronized prostitute in the red-light district. This was a 'secret' to which very few around Boorman's Wells were privy and none dared mention.

The luxurious city life of a high-class lady of the night was liable to rise up and turn on a woman as the years crept by and fresh, girlish charms faded: a sleazier bordello; clients less fastidious about their own bodies and those they used; unhealthy men, mentally as well as physically, with obscene tastes and cruel demands.

In Esther's case, salvation from the dangers she saw looming down trail had come in the lumpy shape of Axel Boorman. He'd offered long-term security in return for marriage to a store- and saloon-keeper. Thus Boorman's Wells had become Esther's refuge, too.

But she was not content to be queen to Axel's king in this piece of semi-desolation.

She was a woman in the prime of life. To Jackson's mind, her alleged fears of decline had had more to do with observing others' fates than the evidence in herself. In Denver, she'd been a pretty girl. Here, a bit more than a handful of years later, she was a beautiful woman. Some slight crinkles at the corner of her deeper, bluer eyes; skin that had taken a tan over parlour pallor; hair with silver threaded through the old auburn tresses now caught up in a bun. But nothing had detracted from a high-cheekboned profile, a full figure and the long, shapely legs a man just knew had to be under the skirts he yearned to raise.

Esther Boorman radiated an almost tangible aura of warmth and desire and invitation. It came from her with every breath she took and every movement she made.

Given rude good health and her past, it was no wonder she had appetites that had led her to drink too freely and regularly cheat on her unappealing husband, so the whispers went.

As though reading Jackson's thoughts, Lil said scowlingly, 'She drinks more'n I do, and she ain't none too careful about lying with men she ain't supposed to. You be careful now.'

Jackson shrugged. 'She's no ordinary woman, I allow.' He could also have added that the man for whom she opened her shapely legs didn't forget the experience.

'No, she's a natural whore if I'm a judge of anything,' Lil said with precocious insight, though she could have no sure knowledge beyond observation of comings and goings in Boorman's absence. 'And you ain't a woman hater or shy of 'em, are you?'

'That's kinda blunt talk for a young lady.'

Taking it further in his head, Jackson's view was that he didn't care for any female temperament. Women had different, distinctly alien intellects from men, with odd exceptions to all the rules, like Misfit Lil whose thought patterns came across as unique in his experience. Accordingly, he shunned closeness with women, though many had tested his resolve over the years. He was aware that Esther might become a temptation, but he'd be ready to haul his freight if that happened.

Misfit Lil made an exasperated, growling sound. 'You ain't taking heed of a word I say, are you? It's a damn disgrace what Mike Covington's reduced you to.'

'Covington means well, Miss Lilian. He's good at heart, but he needs some edges wore off. I've a notion that if you played your cards aright, you'd be the gal to do the chore. You're of an age–'

'God a'mighty! What are you suggesting–? You won't see me cosying up to the crass idiot! He once had the nerve to tell me I needed taming. If he were the last man alive, I'd tell him to go to hell. When it's army business, what he says goes, I guess, but what he done to you ain't fair.'

'Miss Goodnight – life ain't hardly ever fair. You gotta get used to that. You might have a hard time of it, but stand your ground without fuss and you're proved right in the end.'

Lil gave a grunt of contempt. 'You were right already; he was wrong. Paymasters have been travelling across this country since the military first moved in, but I've never heard of Apaches attacking a paymaster and his escort. What can it signify?'

'Yeah...' Jackson sighed. 'There has to be a reason. If we can figger it out, it might save a whole mess of bigger trouble.'

Jackson's next problem was not with the rampaging Apaches but, as Misfit Lil had anticipated, Esther Boorman. Early on, she engineered excuses to be helping him in the rough-and-ready saloon when custom didn't warrant it.

She brushed up close to him in the tight space behind the counter.

'Axel doesn't know we were ... er ... pals in Denver,' she confided. 'We are still friends, aren't we?'

Jackson was acutely aware of the hand that stroked his shoulder and the other that clasped his hip.

'Sure,' he said, in a voice that had more of a husky rasp than he would have liked.

'We could have some fun, you and me, just like the old times in the boarding-house on Market Street.'

'Naw, Esther,' he managed. 'We've left those things buried good and deep behind us.'

But the incorrigible hand at his hip slid further. Only a hypocrite or faintheart could close his mind to the effects, or the charge in the air. Jackson was neither.

'Mmm...' she softly appraised. 'I feel things here that ain't gotten buried. Far from it.'

He pushed her hand off him. 'Esther!' he said with quiet urgency. 'You don't need to make trouble for yourself. You got a good life here. An easy life.'

'Oh, sure ... selling candy to kids and trade goods to pathetic reservation Indians.' She was bitter. 'That's a great life. A healthy gal needs more recreation than a flabby store-owner can give; you know what I mean?'

'Sure. You mean someday when you've got another man in your bed, the door's gonna crash open and the pair of you'll be staring down Boorman's gun barrel.'

'Damned if I need take that for an answer,' she said. 'Or your last word. Give this boring dump a week and it'll eat on you like an acid. Then we'll be of a like mind.'

Despite Esther's confident claim, events showed she didn't set overmuch store by it. They also brought the set-up to crisis point, forcing Jackson to make a decision on his future earlier than he'd intended.

Jackson found Boorman a suspicious, untrusting boss. For instance, he kept locked at all times the back room in which the trading post's reserve stock was kept. Only under his personal supervision were items brought out to replenish what was on display or freshly arrived shipments taken in.

'What does he think I'm gonna do,' Jackson muttered crossly, 'light a shuck into the canyon-lands with a crate of canned peaches tucked under my arm?'

Boorman also wasn't so stupid as to board another man in his own house. Sleeping arrangements for Jackson were that he had his blankets in the hayloft of a rickety barn. Repairing to them in the heat of one afternoon when Boorman was taking his own siesta and the saloon was closed, Jackson found Esther lying in wait for him.

He'd climbed the ladder to the gloom under the rafters. He was wondering whether he shouldn't return to the hard-packed dirt floor, where it was cooler, when his pile of blankets and other gear shifted.

Right off, Jackson was acutely aware of that chilly sense of premonition that told of approaching disaster.

Esther raised herself on to an elbow. The shadows weren't so deep that he couldn't see she was unclothed, at least from the waist up. Beside her, he noted belatedly and absently, stood a bottle he hadn't left here himself. Whether it was half-full or half-empty was something else he was too distracted to consider.

'Jackson,' she said, heavy breasts a-swing and her voice a little thick with whiskey, 'at last you're here. Come and pour me another drink. One for yourself, too.'

'Esther! What the hell d'you think you're doing?'

Seeing her naked, he realized he'd been

wrong about her development into a beautiful woman. She may have gone through such a stage, but now she looked blatantly sultry and over-ripe. Spoiling.

She giggled. 'Oh, don't be a grouch! I should have thought what I'm doing is obvious. Only one way to bring a hesitant man to his senses... You do still find me attractive, don't you? You don't think I'm fat?'

'I think you're no worse than any woman who gets most of her exercise lying on her back and lifting a bottle,' he snarled.

With the half-drunk's uncertain change of mood – wheedling one moment, belligerent the next – her face contorted to show rage and misery.

'Well, I don't give a damn what you think, Mr Farraday. Get on right up here, and perform! Else I'm gonna scream this barn down, so help me God!'

Jackson was trapped. He didn't doubt the crazy woman would carry out her threat. Axel Boorman would come at the run. He was a possessive man; a jealous man. An almighty scene might end in a killing. Only way he could stop it happening would be to knock her senseless. But he didn't hit women.

He also felt sorry for Esther and had

memories of pleasure she'd given him in the past. Besides that, it was months since he'd had a woman, and he was flesh and blood.

So he crawled off the ladder on to the loft planking. Kneeling in the wisps of hay, he gathered up her soft, ready body and kissed her.

'Mmm...' she moaned. 'See? You still like Esther, don't you?'

Her open mouth glued hungrily to his and found his tongue. She worked at his belt with practised fingers.

'You witch,' he complained.

When she'd accomplished her purpose, she broke the kiss, smiled wickedly, and said, 'Now you'll be nice and do your man's work.'

Knowing he couldn't back out till they were done and the insistent urges satisfied, he said gutturally, 'Yeah.'

5

COMINGS AND GOINGS

In a way a cynical observer might have called lovelorn, Misfit Lil had been haunting the environs of Boorman's trading post and spying on Jackson Farraday. She'd built herself a hide in the brush and dead leaves that had been allowed to accumulate under a stand of cottonwood trees between the small settlement and the burnt, yellow and grey hills. Only the keen eyes of a tracker like herself would spot her cleverly concealed little den.

From here, she had an unobstructed view of Boorman's old barn – the sagging doors, the warped and splintered siding bleached colourless by the sun. She could also see Jackson's lamp when he lit it of a night, shining out through the cracks around the high, ill-fitting hay door. Though not much bothered by lonesomeness, it was a comfort to her.

When Lil saw Esther Boorman take herself and her bottle to the barn, she groaned. From amid the confusion of her feelings, she summoned a string of suitable cuss words.

'Bitch! Trollop! Whore!'

She agonized over what she should do. She told herself she was keeping a watch on Jackson Farraday because she felt guilty about her part in obliging him to accept servitude in Boorman's Wells. Jumping into the Angry-fist affair with both feet had been a big mistake.

Now it was plain the randy Esther planned on ambushing Jackson. She'd had more than one lover around Boorman's Wells; anyone filling pants with more than two legs was fair game. For a wonder, Axel Boorman had never caught her at it, since her appetites were conducive to rashness. Lil hoped for Jackson's sake that Esther's luck wasn't about to run out.

Wild schemes for thwarting Esther came to her mind. But most of them would be more likely to raise Boorman from his habitual siesta than help Jackson.

Setting the barn afire appealed mightily – what excitement! – but it would deprive Jackson of a relatively comfortable place to sleep and he might get the blame, too.

Moreover, if Esther had gotten too liquored up to quit before others arrived, it would produce the very questions that needed to be avoided.

And if Esther were to die... Well, murderous thoughts were different from possible responsibility for a murder.

So she sat and watched and fretted. Ten minutes later, Jackson made his way from the saloon to the barn. Neither he nor Esther reappeared.

'They've got together,' she muttered aggrievedly. Should have known it – did know it, she thought. She could always tell right 'uns from wrong 'uns. But she could do nothing, except hope the pair didn't lose all discretion along with their heads. Huffing and scowling, she waited.

This couldn't turn out well.

'Oh God! Oh, Jackson!' Esther said. She arched and thrust her sweaty, slippery body at him. 'More! More!'

Jackson said, 'Haven't you had enough?'

'I don't think I ever want this to end,' she went on breathlessly. 'We must come together again tomorrow. Maybe even tonight, if I can slip Axel something to make him sleep deeply enough...'

63

Jackson grunted. Esther's fevered notions confirmed his worst fears.

'I'm sure you'll try, but I figger you've taken plenty risks for one day. I wouldn't want to – uh – disappoint you, either. Lord, you've worked me dryer than a pump in a drought.'

His mind was already made up. He'd never had much future in Boorman's Wells. With Esther Boorman in the mix, he might not have a future at all. She was insatiable, and like any blackmailer she'd repeat her demands once she'd found how easy a method it was of fulfilling her wants.

One vice Esther had never been short on was greed. She formed a fancy, she had to have it – and aplenty. He was sure it was why she'd turned to prostitution in Denver. Since its incorporation, Denver had been transformed from a crude little town of shacks and tents into the largest city between St Louis and the Pacific Coast. The tenderloin district had legally established boundaries. People were aware of them, and Jackson believed most of the white, Anglo-Saxon girls who resorted to trading themselves on Market Street elected that employment over other courses.

Now, in Boorman's Wells, pleasure itself

was what Esther wanted, having acquired an ineradicable taste for it and the attached excitement and glamour so absent in surroundings she'd wrongly supposed would be her refuge.

'You know you won't disappoint me, Jackson. Why, you're still as servicable as when we started. Tonight you'll be like a rock.'

Jackson tugged himself free of her hugging arms and groped for his stem-winder. He looked at it coldly.

'You're still here when Boorman finishes his siesta, there'll be no tonight for someone.'

'Aww ... let's give it a little longer.'

'No. The fit'll come on again, you'll say the same thing again, if'n you don't swoon. It's time you left.'

She sighed in exasperation. 'All right. But I'll be back for sure.'

She sat up on the tangle of his blankets in sullen silence except for a subsiding harshness of breathing. She brushed the clinging bits of hay from her nakedness, and shook some from her loosened hair. Yet more she picked from a dampened delta of curls. Then she covered the rosy glow of her flesh with her discarded dress and, surprisingly

65

agile and with a wriggle of her plump buttocks, negotiated the ladder.

'Tonight, bravo,' she said.

Jackson feared she'd be as good as her word. He swallowed. Passions were sweeping them into dangerous waters where the pull, like a mighty river's current, would be too strong to resist. Good as the sex might be, it wasn't for him. He'd no doubt what his course had to be. The temptation – the complications it would bring – had to be put behind him pronto.

He waited only till she was gone, then he rolled his blankets and packed his few belongings. The time had come to quit Boorman's Wells.

From her hidey-hole, Misfit Lil watched Esther leave the barn and cross the yard to the trading post and its adjoining living-quarters. She gave a low, knowledgeable laugh. Esther no longer had her bottle, and her gait suggested she'd taken her fill of it and other pleasure.

'The slut!' Lil said, but her voice was tinged with envy. That would have been her strongest feeling if she hadn't also been worried. Axel Boorman must suspect his wife played around, but previously she

66

hadn't done it virtually under his own roof and with an out-and-out employee, though most men hereabouts were beholden to the storekeeper one way or another. Lil reckoned Esther was taking a scary risk with Jackson's life as well as her own.

'You don't want him dead, do you, you silly woman?' she accused softly. 'If Boorman goes off his head, Jackson's blood will be on your soul.'

It was a huge relief when Jackson Farraday appeared but moments later, lugging his saddle and bedroll to the corral where his horse grazed. He was lighting out!

Now that was smart. In her knowledge of men, which was surprisingly extensive for her age, she hadn't met many strong enough to walk away from a situation like this.

Her heart wanted to leap with joy. Yet it didn't. She couldn't believe Jackson was going to be safe. She had a ghastly, intuitive feeling the fat was already in the fire and once it met a hot ember it would flare up.

Axel Boorman, as befitted a man who'd built a business on craft and guile, wasn't so stupid that he hadn't caught the bold and lustful glances his wife tended to throw at the new bar help. But he couldn't discount the possibility he was meant to notice.

Maybe she thought to stoke his own fires somehow. She had appetites polite society didn't openly acknowledge in a woman. Always, he'd found her a demanding, insatiable creature, beautiful, but never getting enough of what she wanted.

Maybe she was setting Farraday up as a decoy, to turn attention from strayings someplace else. He'd suspected for a while she had another man – or men. But who?

When he heard the news late in the day that Jackson Farraday had decamped, he clamped his teeth on the inevitable cigar in his mouth.

'Thought I could trust a man who looked you straight in the eye,' he told Esther. 'So what happened?'

It gave him a heap of sly pleasure to divine that Esther was as irritated by the abrupt and unannounced departure as himself.

'Nothing happened,' she said, too glibly and quickly not to tell him something had. 'He must've had a gutful of a boring job in a damn boring place with nowhere to go.' She shrugged. 'He hightailed it while you were snoring your head off.'

He frowned. Could be her irritation was a mite deeper than he liked.

'Are you giving me lip, woman?'

'No. But just maybe he was a real man and had the right idea. Quitting, I mean.'

He gave her a direct look, meeting her smouldering, resentful gaze and noting the unfamiliar set of determination in her jaw.

He said, 'Are you planning on running out on me?' Suddenly, he thought he could see it all. 'You *knew* he was leaving, didn't you? You're gonna foller him and meet up with him someplace. Like in Denver.'

She laughed at him, but it had a falsity in it. 'You do have an imagination, Axel!'

They were in their bedroom. On a hunch, Boorman reached under the bed and dragged out a carpet-bag.

'Thought as much!' he bellowed in anger. 'Your bag's half-packed already. I figger you got it all fixed with that no-good army scout. You good as admitted he was an old beau.'

'We've got nothing fixed. He knows nothing about my leaving, either. I decided after he left.'

Boorman sneered. 'That's pretty fast thinking. Try telling me you haven't been cheating on me – like the loose, ungrateful hussy you are!'

He upturned the bag over the bed, tipping

out its hastily gathered contents. A ring rolled off the bed, hit the floorboards and bounced. Boorman slammed his boot down on it, picked it up.

His face darkened thunderously as he examined it.

'A gent's gold ring engraved with the initial "J". Lie your way out of this! 'J' for Jackson. Nothing could be plainer. Like as not, you spun him some fancy yarn about undying love. The pair of you were screwing and he gave it you!'

Frantically, she backed away from his spluttering anger.

'It's – old! It has nothing to do with Jackson Farraday. I'll swear it on a Bible!'

Boorman slid open a drawer by the bedside and drew out a six-gun he kept there for protection against nocturnal intruders. He was beside himself with fury over how he'd been cuckolded.

'You're getting no Bible, fornicatress! You're getting your needings!'

Her eyes fixed in wide disbelief on the black eye of the weapon as though she were hypnotized. 'No, Axel, no!' she whimpered. 'Trust me!'

'Hell, You ain't worthy of no trust ever again. I wouldn't trust you far as I could spit. Nobody makes a fool of me!'

'Have mercy on me!'

He laughed without humour. 'I ain't built a whole damn settlement and business on a reputation for being soft.'

He had her in a corner of the small room, away from door and window. Trapped. And he was incensed beyond reason. His mind was filled with the crazy image of her riding his absconded bar-help. She was astride, cowgirl fashion, improbably impaled on the horn of her workbench.

His gun boomed.

The single, close shot took Esther in the stomach, below her ample bosom. She rose up on her toes, head thrown back in agony and her voluptuous body arched one last time. Then she collapsed to her knees, mouth working in soundless gasps and the blood spilling from her body.

Boorman saw the heavy slug had torn right through her, leaving a jagged exit wound and spattering the wall behind with pieces of torn tissue and a trickling arc of blood that traced the line of her fall.

On the floor, Esther twisted and writhed, her hands clasped over the spurting, breath-stopping wound. She'd gone into shock and it wasn't apparent whether she was conscious, though her eyes were open and staring.

Sanity returned to Boorman on the wave of horror that washed over him at the sight of the rapidly dying woman.

Goddamnit! He'd actually shot her, *killed* the promiscuous, beautiful woman he'd taken for a wife. He was seized by instant remorse. How did he get out of this?

The shot would have been heard. Folks were liable to come a-running and asking questions. What could he do, outside of confess, and plead the extreme provocation of a libidinous, straying spouse who'd kept the incentive for most everything she did in her loins?

He wasn't given much time to think. From outside came a husky cry.

'Boorman! Axel Boorman! What goes on in there?'

Blast it, of all times...! The wheezing voice was that of the Silver Vein sheriff, Willard Skene, due to make one of his regular visits.

6

SCHEMING 'WHEEZER' SKENE

The shot brought Misfit Lil, dozing in her bivouac in the cottonwoods, instantly alert. She wasn't the only one. The Boorman's Wells riff-raff were gathering outside the log-built trading post.

And pushing them aside after hitching his horse to the rail out front was Sheriff Willard 'Wheezer' Skene. Whether she felt happy about this, she didn't know. His arrival might prove opportune. It might not. Depended on what had happened and what the meaning was of the single shot. Skene had been her nemesis for many a fun-producing bit of mischief she'd instigated.

She considered him moronic and beastly. Once, he'd invited her to spend a night privately in his rooms in town in exchange for overlooking to inform her pa how she'd done up the town on a high-spirited Saturday night. It was therefore hard to have pity for him, although he suffered chronic asthma.

This curse was what had brought him to the country, seeking a cure which had been denied him by virtue of dust and weed pollen.

As she'd once boldly told him, Skene 'hurt her ears, offended her nose, and disgusted her eyes'.

Skene surged into the Boormans' place and seconds later came back out almost as quickly. He had a spell of impressive coughing before he got control of his vocal cords and calmed himself.

'All right. Back off, the lot o' yuh!' he rasped.

Misfit Lil imagined his lungs pumping like an old bellows, the dry leather cracking and creaking.

'Ain't nothin' yuh can do straight off, folks,' he continued. 'But stick around. I figger yuh might be called on.'

With these ominous words, he went back into the home.

Lil knew he was a frequent caller on Axel Boorman. In her shrewd way – she had an inkling of most rascality that went on in Skene's bailiwick – she reckoned he collected from the store and saloon keeper more than the taxes and fees that were his legal entitlement for the supplement of his sheriff's salary.

Despite his ailment, Skene practised autocracy and opportunism to profitable effect. He'd have his eyes on Boorman's local wealth for sure. She knew that at one time he'd also had them on the sensual Esther, though she'd reason to believe his coughing and wheezing had made him unacceptable to the saloon man's wife, howsoever catholic her tastes in liaisons.

Agog with curiosity, she dropped to her stomach, flattened herself to the earth and wriggled to a point closer to the big cabin of the trading post. She chose the biggest bush and slithered into its cover. From here, she was as in as good a position as the small waiting crowd to witness what might eventuate. Meantime, she could listen to the speculation, which was mighty interesting in itself.

Axel Boorman had gone quickly from aggressive, aggrieved husband to quivering wreck. He couldn't stop his hands from shaking. He was consumed by a huge sense of loss – and fear.

'Here, take this, Axel. Swallow it down.' Skene pressed a bottle of the post's best bonded whiskey into his trembling clutch.

'I killed her, Willard,' he sobbed. 'Couldn't

take it no more. She had this ring offa Jackson Farraday. She was gonna foller him to Denver, I know it. She sent me plumb loco with her smug lying and her cheating. I shot her dead. Never seen so much blood.... You'll have to arrest me for murder. I'll hang!'

'No, yuh won't, yuh damned fool,' Skene croaked. 'Pull yourself together. Ain't no way I c'n allow yuh to stand trial on account o' that no-account tramp. All your rackets'd be apt to be exposed. The tradin' in forbidden goods – like that rotgut whiskey to the Apaches. Not to dare mention the bigger stuff we got planned.'

Boorman nodded, his misery deepening. 'Yeah, Willard, I know. I've let you down real bad. The payoffs'll be over when I'm gone.'

'Chris'sakes, man, stop yuh snivellin', will yuh? An' lissen ... it ain't gonna be that way. I dassn't let it. I ain't lettin' yuh cost me my job and my name, see?'

Boorman was bewildered. 'But this finishes us, Willard. I've ruined the game–'

'Bullshit! The game's scarce begun. We got big dollars comin' our way, remember?'

'Not any more.'

'Sure we have. This ain't nothin' but a hiccup. You'll accuse Farraday of the crime. He robbed yuh of the saloon and store takings, killed Esther and went on the dodge.'

'I d-don't know that I'm up to that, Willard,' Boorman stammered.

Skene tapped the butt of his holstered Colt revolver meaningfully.

'Yuh'll have to be, or I'll see yuh're a dead man afore yuh get to any trial. We ain't havin' no enquiries or tale-tellin' around here.'

Misfit Lil was tiring of the boring conjectures of the handful of deadbeats who led their lives of boredom and drudgery in the environs of Boorman's Wells. One wild notion was that Angry-fist, or one of his followers, had broken into the trading post and been shot dead or, alternatively, had shot Boorman.

The theory was exploded when the store owner appeared on the veranda closely behind Willard Skene, but he looked pallid and the cigar in his mouth drooped a mite soggily.

The sheriff raised his arms to quieten the hubbub and Lil strained her ears.

'Mrs Boorman's bin murdered,' he wheezed harshly. 'She was shot by Jackson Farraday, who's stolen the saloon takings from Axel's safe an' lit out for Denver. We gotta raise a posse and git after the bastard!'

Lil could scarcely contain her indignation. That was crazy-talk. Outright lies. The single shot had come considerable time after she'd seen Jackson leave. He hadn't been hurrying as a fugitive might. More like going quietly and cautiously. Nor had he looked provisioned for any trip to Denver, which was way across the territorial border – 300 miles even as the straightest crow could fly, many more paralleling the course of the Colorado River.

But Esther Boorman dead! That, too, was stunning, yet not hard for her to understand. She'd either killed herself, or her husband had killed her. Probably the latter. For reasons of his own, Wheezer Skene was protecting Boorman and framing Jackson.

Lil, driven as much by impulse as reason, since such was her nature, almost leaped up and denounced the crooked sheriff. But in time she realized that would serve no good. Credibility for a girl with the reputation she had wouldn't be high, and how could she explain why she was spying on Jackson Farraday without making herself look a poor little fool?

No point in getting your blood in a boil, Lil my girl, she told herself, and pondered her other options.

The Wells folks – many of whom Misfit Lil regarded as failed scoundrels or soft-brains – crowded around Skene and Boorman, pressing them with questions.

'Shuddup!' Skene croaked. 'We can't waste time standin' here an' chewin' the rag. Fetch your hosses, saddle up, the lot o' yuh. I'm deputizin' y'all to ride down that murderin' Jackson Farraday an' bring him in, dead or alive!'

The bunch scattered to wherever their saddle stock was corralled or stabled. In moments, they were drifting back armed with an assortment of shotguns, rifles and pistols. Skene was champing at the bit to ride, itching to get after his scapegoat.

Lil noted the unprofessional nature of the posse that formed up; the sad overall quality of its horseflesh.

'Crowbait!' she murmured in disdain, taking what small heart she could. Her own pony was a sleek, powerful animal that would have no trouble outriding such a posse.

For this was what she had to do – find Jackson's tracks ahead of them, hunt him down first, and warn him of the danger he was in.

Still unseen, she wormed back to the hide, and to the glade among the trees where she'd picketed her horse.

Jackson Farraday considered himself well out of the trouble Esther had been brewing for him at Boorman's Wells. He jogged his horse without pushing it along the trail to Silver Vein. The easy pace put the pleasant, familiar breeze of the rolling countryside in his face. Not since he'd set out after Angry-fist with Lieutenant Covington's detachment had he felt in such a relaxed frame of mind.

Working at the trading post had been a bad move. The reunion with Esther might have been compensatory, had it not been for her changed status to married woman. From the start, it had been more than she could do to keep from throwing herself on him; a recipe for disaster if ever he saw one.

He veered his big sorrel toward some yellow aspens, shading red and black rocks. He was in no hurry and stopped momentarily to watch the swoop and climb of two gopher hawks in the evening sky. Given the lateness of the hour, he could make a good, sheltered camp here before night fell.

Later, squatting on his heels by a small cook-fire and sipping a tin cup of hot coffee, the pound of hoofbeats came to him through the dusk. The rider had left the roadway and was heading straight for his makeshift camp. Warily, he placed his right hand on the butt of his holstered Colt. He squinted through the trees.

'Jackson Farraday! Is that you back there?'

He recognized the voice that raised the cry instantly.

'Lilian Goodnight, by all that's holy! D'you make a habit of riding in on folks' camps?'

Misfit Lil rode from the grey shadows into the small circle of flickering firelight. She was in a state of some agitation.

'No, I do not, Mr Farraday,' she replied respectfully, to his terse question.

'Aah, mebbe it's only when you fancy free coffee then?'

'Don't try to make fun of me, Mr Farraday, please. I'm here to save your life!'

'Oh...' Jackson said, fingering his neat chin-beard in puzzlement. 'What kind of tall tale is this?'

Lil's fists clenched in exasperation on the reins of her pony. 'It's no windy, just the plain truth. Esther Boorman has been shot dead and the word put around that the trading post was robbed. Wheezer Skene is framing you. He formed a posse and they're out to get you, dead or alive.'

81

'Esther killed!'

The news was startling; almost unbelievable. Only hours previously she had been so full of life and passion. But she had also been on a path to likely ruin. It was just that he hadn't realized how imminent the end was.

'Deader 'n a doornail, mister. Murdered. And you gotta ride out of this country afore they catch up. It's only 'cos most of 'em are piss-poor horsemen on sway-backed, broken-down cayuses that I've gotten to you first. Stamp out your fire and saddle up!'

Jackson's thoughts were running fast. He studied the girl's honest face and saw no signs of trickery or mischief-making. He didn't share the popular conception of her as a scallywag. She was a nuisance, but she had local knowledge and a talent for outdoors life that would be the envy of many a trail-hardened man. She seemed honestly worried. Excitement tinged her voice when she spoke and her eyes glittered with the sense of danger she felt. They were never still, flashing glances in every direction as she looked – and listened with sudden tilts of her head – for the first tell-tale signs of a pursuit.

He didn't consider it in any way vital to ask at this time how she knew he hadn't shot

Esther Boorman. Misfit Lil came and went about business that was often a mystery to all but herself. It was part of her largely unrecognized skills that she witnessed what others missed.

He frowned. 'It's coming full dark and no time to go on the dodge.'

'But the stars are brightening and the moon will be nigh full when it rises.'

Beyond the fireglow, the darkness under the trees and among the rocks was growing impenetrable.

'Fine,' he said, nodding. 'So we stay put and real still until it does.'

'All right,' she agreed reluctantly. 'Maybe they'll miss your tracks where you swung off the trail and ride on by. They reckon you're headed for Denver.'

Only moments after she spoke, they heard the lumbering approach of the posse and the shouts that passed between the men as they picked their way along the roadway in the darkness.

Misfit Lil clasped a hand over her horse's muzzle to stop it from whickering a greeting to the posse's animals. 'Your horse,' she hissed, but Jackson was already moving to the side of the picketed sorrel.

The threat of discovery passed and a rising

pale moon grew in intensity. Soon the grove of aspens was bathed in soft light.

'Time to ride out,' Lil said, and swung lithely into her saddle. 'Where will you go?'

'I think I'll hole up in the canyonlands, taking my chances on running a-foul of Angry-fist and his Apaches. Wait till the dust settles, so to speak, before I move on to fresher pastures. There has to be some mistake for 'em all to reckon I robbed Boorman and killed Esther. Mebbe the truth will get out somehow.'

'And if it doesn't?'

He shrugged his broad shoulders and shook his long-haired head, but kept his voice flat and his face expressionless.

'No knowing. It'll be my problem, not yours.'

Lil decided abruptly, 'You'll need a pard, a sidekick free to come and go and keep you posted. I'll ride along with you, Mr Farraday, so I know where you're hiding.'

'That, young lady, is a damn-fool notion if I ever heard one. Why don't you get on home to the Flying G, less'n some galoot gets wind you passed me the word on the posse?'

Misfit Lil was scornful. 'Huh! I can handle that kinda trouble, and they can't hang or shoot me for killing Esther Boorman.'

'Godamighty! You really are the peskiest, stubbornest female I ever come across.' Then, with a hint of mockery, he added, 'Ain't no wonder Mike Covington'll have no dealings with you.'

'Don't drag that uppity stuffed shirt into this! We need the military like a hole in the head.'

They tossed the developing argument between them as they regained the roadway and open country, but it wasn't Jackson or Lil's fault that the hunters and the hunted spotted each other simultaneously.

Plumes of dust rose ghostly white in the moonlight from a series of black dots on the horizon that rapidly formed into a straggling group of riders. Suddenly, wild yells broke out as the posse-men caught a first glimpse of them across the flat miles of grassland. They broke straightaway into a charge, kicking unmercifully at flagging mounts to get as much speed out of them as possible.

'Jesus! They must've realized they'd lost your trail and turned back,' Lil said. 'We gotta run our hosses like the wind!'

7

PRINCESS OF PISTOLEERS

A thin, asthmatic wail was borne on the night air to Jackson and Lil.

'Stop, or yuh're buzzard bait!'

Lil laughed. 'Skene is a bag of whistling wind! Our horses are better and fresher. Once we reach the canyons, we'll lose them in the darkness.'

But spent bullets kicked up puffs of dust around them, and when they looked back they saw moonlight glint on belching long guns which several over-eager possemen had drawn from their scabbards.

Jackson knew the odds were stacked against him. Was Misfit Lil right to trust in their slim advantage of the better mounts?

In the event, it came down to superior riding skills and knowledge of the country that unfolded under their horses' flying hoofs in the darkness of moon shadows. Jackson was forced to admit to himself an admiration for his young companion's ability to handle herself and her horse. She was an extraordinary girl, for sure.

Their flight into higher, rockier parts led to a stretch of badlands.

'We've shaken 'em off, it seems like,' Jackson said. 'I reckon it's best now we should make camp till daybreak. You savvy that?'

'Sure,' Lil said. 'I savvy you, Mr Farraday. It'd be a fool thing for either of us to break a horse's leg. What's more, we're close by the last waterhole for many miles.'

Jackson guessed she, like their horses, was already suffering from a lack of water. She was even less prepared than he for a long journey. He knew by the state he was in himself that dust and grit from their gruelling ride would have worked under her clothing and would be chafing her skin. Most other women he'd known would have been demanding a hot, deep tub.

He was reminded of Esther, the Denver prostitute who'd fitted so badly into this environment – and of her depressingly wretched end, laid at his door.

They rested up watchfully, taking turns to doze, in a natural, elevated amphitheatre surrounded on three sides by parapets of brown rock. Besides having water, the place was a virtual fortress. To the fourth, north side was a steep slope of shale that terminated in a yawning drop into an effectively inaccessible canyon. When they'd approached their resting place by a precarious trail on the edge of the shale, the horses had been stiff-necked and bulging-eyed. Only their trust in their riders had kept the spooked and tired creatures from balking at the last climb.

At first light, Jackson roused himself properly, knowing they had to be on their way before the inept posse was able to use what tracking skill it possessed to locate them. He was shocked to find Misfit Lil missing. Only a small heap of dumped clothing, including undergarments, lay where he'd last seen her.

Sounds of splashing ended his momentary alarm. She was bathing in the spring-fed water-hole, hidden by the boulders that bordered it.

Lil heard his small movements. 'Ready to ride, are we?' she sang out, and tripped into his sight, making no attempt to conceal her wet nakedness.

She made a lively nymph, athletically proportioned and tall for a girl. Almost as tall as Jackson himself. The plump globes of her bosom were small but a perfect pair. She had a narrow waist and hips, firm buttocks and fine, strong legs. Dark hair hung in dripping tresses over alabaster shoulders that presented a stark contrast to her sun-bronzed face and neck. She made no attempt to cover her most secret charms, but the symmetrical whole was a delight and the total absence of clothing effaced any suggestion of rudeness. The effect was of innocence.

She had none of the shame or embarrassment most respectable girls of her age and time were wont to show when stumbled across naked. The conventional society in which Jackson had been brought up regarded women's genitals as 'the shameful parts', and clerics preached that female sexuality was synonymous with shame.

Lil squeezed water from her hair, shook her head, as an animal might, and said, 'You're gaping, Mr Farraday. I know you've seen a woman before. Quit it, please, before I think you fool-headed.'

'Miss Goodnight, it ain't decent to tempt or tease any man thisaway. Were I a man without scruples you'd be in pure trouble showing yourself like you have.'

Lil sighed. 'You think I don't know *that?*'

Moments later, satisfied with her state of dryness and still undismayed at all she artlessly flaunted, Lil was pulling on her clothing. Jackson, quickly saddled up and about ready to go, was fiddling a mite self-consciously at putting on his hat, when a high-powered rifle whip-cracked below them.

The hat sailed away from his hands and head.

Before a second bullet whined through the space that had been occupied by his head, he and Lil ducked for cover below the parapet of their high hideout.

'Hell, that was close!' Jackson said. His seven-and-a-half-inch Frontier Colt filled his big fist.

'They must've sneaked up on us while I was bathing,' Lil complained, pulling on the last of her mannish duds. 'That'll teach me to want to smell clean like a lady.'

'You could've gotten stinky as all get-out for what I care. Our tails are in a crack now.'

From below a voice yelled, 'This posse's got yuh surrounded, Farraday. Throw out your weapons, come on down an' face your deservings, yuh blackhearted, yeller-livered woman-killer! Likewise the feller yuh got up thar helpin' yuh. A piece o' treacherous trash for sure, ridin' with a murderer.'

Lil exulted proudly, 'The bastards still

don't know it's me who warned you.'

But Jackson was unhappy. 'I'm not giving myself up to a crazy lynch mob. The way I see it, we're gonna have us a wild shootout. I plumb wish you weren't here.'

'You don't say? Well, that's gratitude,' Lil said.

'Wishing anything else is wishing you dead.'

She was indignant. 'The Silver Vein folks don't call me the Princess of Pistoleers for nothing!'

Jackson knew about that, but a full-scale gun siege was in prospect, and he didn't want responsibility for drawing her into it on his head.

He had an admiration for her, of sorts, could even grow to like her if she weren't so damned confrontational and self-reliant to the point of foolhardiness. He looked at her as he might on seeing someone for the first or last time: a dark-haired, spry girl with expressive grey eyes, her face animated, too, by little changes flickering around her mouth – by turns humorous and grave as the spirit moved her.

'Farraday! Yuh hear us? Yuh come on down, both. And with your hands lifted!'

It was Wheezer Skene, straining his voice but managing to make every word heard. A more bullish voice added, 'We got the guns. You're outnumbered an' trapped. We don't want to have to kill that other *hombre*. You're the one we want.'

A third man said, 'We can smash yuh to bits. Be like bashing unwanted kittens in a sack!'

What was Jackson to do? Surrender and die? Engage in a gun battle that might end in another innocent party's death as well as his own?

Misfit Lil provided the answer. She bobbed up and let rip with her six-shooter in the direction of the threat. An anguished yelp told everyone she'd got lucky, or was extremely quick-eyed.

An answering hail of lead bounced and whined off the rocks all around Jackson and Lil, but the girl had already ducked down into shelter. Stone chips and splinters and chips stung their exposed faces, necks and backs of hands.

'Back off,' Jackson snapped at Lil. 'Get away from here. I'll hold 'em off. Try to work down the shale slope.'

'Nope,' she said tersely, as the echoes of the ricochets died. 'I'm as good a shot as you. 'Sides, I know the trail out that way is narrow to the point of suicide, specially for a body in a hurry.'

Exasperated at her refusal to do as she was told, Jackson rose up himself and fired his Colt from their ridge toward a rugged area strewn with rocks and boulders where he thought the attackers were. They'd left their horses down the trail apiece and were climbing on foot toward their now unsafe sanctuary.

A posseman, threading his way among the rocks, was panicked by Jackson's fire. Flushed out of his cover, he made a zig-zagging retreat, crouching low.

Jackson took careful aim and fired a second time. He thought he heard the bullet strike flesh a split-second after the Colt's crash. The man was spilled off his feet and rolled, clutching his holed limb and screaming.

'Aargh! The bastard's busted m' leg!'

Again, the reverberating roar of many rifles shattered the dawn in frenzied response.

Jackson heard Lil gasp. He thought her upper arm had been grazed by a ricochet, but she gritted her teeth at the hurt. Popping up once more, she picked a target – a scrap of coloured fabric edging a boulder – and proved again she was an excellent markswoman.

'This is much too much!' Jackson rapped,

bracing for the inevitable response, a cascade of potentially deadly lead and shards of rock.

Over his shoulder, he glimpsed his sorrel rear up where it was tethered close to the waterhole. Had it been hit? It seemed not. It made a run for the tortuous trail by which they'd reached the place, followed by Lil's pony. He hoped Skene's attackers wouldn't shoot them down.

About then, the posse decided to storm their citadel, all guns firing ... and Jackson decided he had only one way left to save Lil from the sorry mess. Maybe she'd go if he went.

He lurched to his feet and set off, head ducked, on a weaving run, boulder to boulder, for the dangerous slope of loose shale.

Behind him, the yelling and shooting rose to a crescendo. Lead whipped past his head; more sent up spouts of dust only inches from his boots.

Skene's rag-tag company had screwed up its courage and was coming in a charge, smoking rifles, carbines and shotguns in hand, relying on force of numbers.

Misfit Lil shouted, 'Hey, come back, you lousy quitter! You'll kill yourself going that way!'

'Follow me!' he shouted.

But she shook her head vigorously, having none of it.

Misfit Lil was disappointed to see Jackson break off the fight. She would never have expected Jackson Farraday to run out on a comrade-in-arms.

She saw him swerve, then take a headlong dive, rolling against the base of a rock at the very edge of the slope, scrabbling to get a hold on it. Her heart leaped to her mouth. It looked very much like he might have stopped a posse slug.

But she couldn't afford to pause and watch. She had her own life to save, and knew it. Moreover, she'd used her last shot and didn't waste time trying to reload.

A Boorman's Wells deadbeat, built big like a grizzly, hauled himself over the parapet of rock in front of her. The cocked pistol he had at the ready dropped, even as did his jaw, when he saw he was confronted by a girl.

'By God! It's Misfit L–'

Lil kicked the pistol from the surprised posse-man's fist. Simultaneously, holding her emptied Colt by the hot barrel, she surged forward and swung the full weight of the butt and chamber into his brutal face. The crunch of iron into the bone of his nose was followed by a satisfying spurt of blood. He staggered from the swift clout and went down, flailing and moaning.

She straightened, breathing hard and wiping sweat, hair, rock dust and a little blood out of her eyes. She felt more blood trickling down her sleeve from the sore graze on her upper arm.

A first sunbeam threw a glint off a tin badge pinned to a vest. Coming up behind the downed posseman, and covering her with his rifle, Sheriff Skene rasped, 'That's enough! We got yuh, kid. Put down that gun!'

'Might as well. It's empty. If'n it weren't, and it came to a shootout, you wouldn't have a prayer.'

Skene realized who they'd flushed out. '*You!* I mighta guessed it. A meddlin' bitch of a wildcat, aidin' and abettin' a dangerous fugitive!'

'You're a dirty liar, Wheezer Skene. I'll tell the world Jackson Farraday was innocent.'

'Grab her! She ain't talkin' her way outa nothin'. I'm gonna put her in the Silver Vein hoosegow. An' her pa'll have to raise hefty bail afore she gits out this time.'

Two of the possemen Skene had deputized took a cruel grasp of her arms. Neither cared a jot that her left sleeve was torn and bloodstained. Conversely, she took pleasure to note that one of the approaching bunch had a blood-soaked neckerchief around his upper arm and his shirt was stiffening with coagulated blood. She reckoned this was the man she'd winged first; that she'd taken a bigger chunk of flesh out of his arm.

Skene jabbed the muzzle of his rifle into her ribs. He looked around warily, eyes slitted. 'Where is he? Where's Farraday?'

'Find out your ownselves, you bunch of no-accounts!'

Skene whacked a meaty hand across her rump. 'Yuh're askin' for a larrupin', gal!'

'Give you pleasure to beat a gal's ass black and blue wouldn't it, you pervert?'

A posseman with a vestige of respect for propriety put the exchange back on course.

'Farraday went over that thar edge.'

Axel Boorman trudged up, a damp, much-chewed stogie stuck in his mouth. 'Did he get away then?' he asked anxiously, a cold sweat beading his pasty face.

'Naw. Reckon he's dead. Riddled like a sieve to boot, I'd figger.'

The whole party went to the far side of the

amphitheatre, dragging Lil with them. They reached the north rim and studied the shale slope carefully, eyes straining to make out details. The early light of day hadn't yet reached far enough to give a clear picture but a gouged channel ran through the shale to the drop-off where the slope turned vertical and plunged hundreds of feet into the dark depths of the canyon.

'Where's his body then?' Boorman bleated.

Skene laughed evilly. 'Way down where we ain't gonna bother to find it, even if we could. What could be better, Axel ol' friend?' He thumped him on the back, but the trading post boss didn't seem to appreciate it any more than Lil had her slapped backside.

She felt devastated. The hollow in her stomach was more than hunger for a missed breakfast. Jackson Farraday, dead and gone. She didn't want to believe it.

8

TWO IN TROUBLE

'You can't just ride out of here. Suppose he's down there someplace, injured, dying...' Misfit Lil protested.

'Waal, ain't that jest too bad, sister,' Skene said. His eyes gleamed with derision, and something else. 'The rat got his comeuppance, I'd say. An' yuh gonna git yourn when I git yuh back to my jail!'

They hustled her back to their waiting horses, where they lashed her wrists behind her back with part of a broken leather strap from a saddle's rigging and boosted her none too delicately on to Skene's horse in front of him. He chuckled, his face wreathed in dirty smiles.

Lil found the rough manhandling humiliating, and the closeness of the crooked sheriff's body when it was done was abhorrent, especially since he wrapped his left arm round her chest and held her firm and steady with a groping hand. She was acutely aware of her body's involuntary responses to the cruel treatment; the fingers that pinched her.

She was seized by an impotent, consuming rage.

'Don't let the pig get away with any of this, you men!' she cried. 'Jackson Farraday didn't kill Esther Boorman. He was her good friend in Denver.'

'Yeah, we 'preciate that,' a black-bearded posse-man said drily. 'Mebbe his motive were more'n a cash-money robbery ... mebbe he wanted to git back inta her drawers an' she turned him down.'

'That's a ridiculous suggestion!' Lil retorted. 'Esther was chasing *him*. Mr Farraday is unlike some here, who haven't a decent bone in their bodies. He's all man – handsome and with manners and true grit.'

Another of the Wells crowd sniggered. 'Uh-huh! I reckon yuh had one o' them girlish passions for the bastard... Seen him as a kinda knight of the range, like in a Walter Scott romance, was that it?'

Skene wheezed, 'Ain't gonna be no pretty fairy tales where she's headed.'

The picture came unbidden to Lil's mind of Jackson Farraday riding carelessly well, like a cavalier, with his long hair flowing out in the wind behind him. She felt an unfamiliar sensation of warmth in her cheeks and wondered if she'd reddened to the roots of her hair, like the fairskinned Eastern girls in Boston whom she'd initiated into womanhood with the co-operation of the shameless gardener's-boy.

'It was nothing like that!' she declared vehemently, but to general laughter.

'Yuh'll grow up an' outa it someday, Miss Goodnight,' said one of the less obnoxious members of the posse.

She said stiffly, but with moistness coming to her eyes, 'Mr Farraday was honourable. I'll feel the same way about him always – today, tomorrow and forever!'

The laughter was as raucous and unsympathetic as before.

The Princess of Pistoleers held no fears for them now. With her Colt empty and stuck in Skene's belt, the hellcat's fangs were drawn. Nor could bluster and braggadocio, of which she was an able practitioner, be of service to her in her belittling predicament.

The man with the black beard licked his lips and said, 'Damnit, Willard, I'd sure like to help yuh give the proud bitch what's comin' to her when we git to town.'

'You daren't lay a molesting finger on me,

mister,' Lil said, though her voice wobbled, and Skene continued without check to grope and squeeze her chest exploringly as his horse jogged along with its double load. 'Why, I'd tell my father, Ben Goodnight, and that'd cook your goose!'

Skene laughed. 'Way I know it, ol' Ben ain't too likely these days to credit the tales yuh might tell, missy. Ain't much weight in your say-so anyplace.'

Into her ear he added in a raspy whisper, 'An' we'll put our fingers an' whatever wheresoever we like, leavin' not a broken scrap of evidence. I do hear tell yuh ain't been a virgin since yuh was sent back from the East....'

The threat hung in the rapidly heating air as they descended to the plains, which already shimmered in a summer haze. Yet Lil felt a cold shudder of repulsion go through her body. For a few awful moments she thought she was going to faint. The world reeled in dizzying circles. If her stomach wasn't so empty, she was sure Skene's advising of her dread fate would have made her throw up right there over the mane of his plodding horse.

'I'm not a whore, Sheriff Skene,' she finally managed to say.

Skene rejected that with the smug assertion of a common belief of his century's thinkers. 'Every gal who yields to her passions and loses her virtue is a prostitute.'

When Jackson Farraday threw himself at the base of the rock on the rim that divided the amphitheatre from the shale slope, it was not because he was hit by the lead of Skene's dirty law.

He pulled himself in behind its cover to plan a daring descent that would ultimately take him all the way to the canyon floor, breathtakingly far below. He also still hoped that Lil, fearless as she was under gunfire, would follow his example and break off the fight, or at the very least not throw away her life on his behalf.

He waited several moments, but she didn't come.

Much as Misfit Lil knew about this country – her country – he began to realize that she didn't know all he knew. Probably likely vice versa. A channel fissured the canyon face, little wider than a man's body. Though he'd never tested it, it might be possible for a determined fellow to brace himself within the crack and ease himself down. The back of his shirt and trousers would get torn to shreds, the soles and heels of his boots holed or broken, his hands cut and sore till the blood ran. But just maybe he'd make it to the bottom alive.

First, however, he had to negotiate the shale. Once it started sliding, he'd go with it and never locate the fissure.

Gingerly, he edged downslope. At one point, he dislodged a large chunk of rock. It went end over end, carving a groove through the smaller shale till it hurtled over the lower edge. Many seconds later, he heard it crash into the brush that lined the canyon bottom. It had been a big rock; it made little noise. Both that and elapsed time confirmed the entire fall had to be measured in many hundreds of feet.

Jackson remembered the fissure terminated between two distinctive, gaunt prominences that overhung the canyon, seeming to menace any who passed below.

He headed carefully for where the contours seemed to correspond with what he could remember. A first stroke of luck! He'd made the right choice between a couple of possibilities. This was the place.

Fortunately, little shale had lodged on the lower edge of the slope. Smaller rocks that slid that far then presumably continued right on, hurtling out into the empty air, as Jackson would if he put a foot wrong.

Kneeling on the edge with his back to the dizzying fall below, he lowered down himself into the fissure. He was resting up after his exertions, when he heard the voices above discussing his supposed fate.

'Farraday went over that thar edge...'

'Reckon he's dead. Riddled like a sieve to boot, I'd figger.'

The voices came closer, but to his relief, he must have been shielded from his hunters' sight by the overhanging rock and they weren't game to venture on to the slope of shale.

'Where's his body then?'

'Way down where we ain't gonna bother to find it, even we could...'

The sounds of the posse receded. Mixed among the voices, he thought he could hear Misfit Lil's. He made out no distinct words, but it gladdened him to know she was possibly still alive, till he thought of the hands she would be in.

He hadn't heard yet of the man who'd monkeyed with Misfit Lil and not got the worst of it, but Willard Skene and Axel Boorman were seemingly ready to foist blame for Esther's death on him with nary a skerrick of real evidence – wanting him dead no less – and the suggestion in this was that they were more ruthless men than he'd suspected.

He felt bitter. Much as he turned it over in his mind, none of it made complete sense to him ... yet.

It took Jackson a gruelling hour of painful, shuffling effort to lower himself to the canyon floor.

When he'd made it, a long hike awaited him, his route determined by waterholes and the breaks and folds of the forbidding landscape rather than any straight line back to the nearest outpost of civilization. Too, he had to admit that his descent of the canyon face hadn't left him in the best shape for the trek.

The canyon bottom was uneven and at a higher altitude than the plains. It was still goat's work scrambling down from the badlands, but in the foothills, the fates looked kindly on Jackson for a second time. He emerged from the desolation into a meadow less parched than the wider terrain to see his sorrel grazing unconcerned and unharmed. The beast had evidently evaded the posse and thought better of cantering back to Silver Vein or Boorman's Wells.

He snuck up on the horse, fearing it might

be spooked by his dishevelled and wild appearance, but when he drew close it raised its head and saw him. He stopped instantly and gave a low whistle. He was relieved when the horse responded obediently by coming to meet him. All was now far from lost. He noted that though he'd forfeited his bedroll, abandoned at the campsite battle scene, his saddle was secure and his near-new Winchester still sat in its scabbard, slung under the stirrup leathers. He'd also gained a full canteen of water.

'Good gal,' Jackson said, rubbing the horse's nose.

He heaved himself into the saddle and set off at a steady, rocking-horse lope, hoofs hammering the hard ground. He felt close to exhaustion, but he wanted to reassure himself that Lilian Goodnight was safe, and somehow set enquiries afoot into the evil business that had turned him into a fugitive.

What game were Skene and Boorman playing?

Distracted by his thoughts and his fatigue, Jackson was shocked when, in answer to reawakening sixth sense, he glanced up and saw a line of bronzed horsemen had topped out on a rocky rim to his left and were keeping pace with him. It was as though they'd materialized wraithlike from the harsh magnificence of the terrain.

Angry-fist and his band of excitable young bucks!

They could be no others. The redmen who lived on the reservation largely wore white man's garb, favouring round-crowned black hats and jackets and pants of denim, duck or similar hard-wearing material. These emulated their charismatic, hotheaded leader and went almost naked except for their breech-clouts.

Angry-fist himself stood out among them. Either gaining in stature or in self-aggrandisement, he'd adorned his black hair with a plumed head-dress in place of his headband and eagle's feather. A necklace of teeth and claws was around his neck, and beaded armlets encircled his muscular biceps.

Observing that his party was seen, Angry-fist checked his mount, dragging it back on its haunches. He flourished a feathered war lance above his head. In obedience to a barked command, his followers put their heels into the ribs of their fleet-footed mustangs and streamed down a path from the high ridge, whooping ferociously as they came.

Jackson kicked his sorrel into a gallop

Shots whistled past his head in quick succession. The Apaches had familiarized themselves with the new, Army-issue repeating rifles doubtless taken from the ambushed paymaster's slain escort.

A lock of Jackson's streaming hair was clipped off, but that could have been a lucky – or unlucky – shot. It seemed they didn't want him to die quickly, judging by the number that passed closely yet missed. The bizarre thought occurred to him that maybe his scalp was especially prized and they wanted to lift it intact.

Apaches! Until very recently, they'd been the feared, deadly masters of the South-West. Though outnumbered and outgunned, and chased and harassed from one end of the territories to the other, they'd still managed to make fools of their enemies – including the army. Angry-fist was a throwback with designs of similar kind, and would have recognized him as the army's chief scout and tracker in this country.

Grimly, Jackson reflected that next to killing, torture was a skill the Apache excelled in. He'd seen some of their vicious handiwork with the knife.

He clapped the sides of his broken boots to the hard-pressed sorrel.

9

FATES WORSE THAN DEATH

Angry-fist's braves reached the flat in a last wild scramble of rolling stones and crumbling earth under their ponies' hoofs.

Jackson was racing for his life. Turning in the saddle and bracing himself against the cantle with his left hand, he raised his Frontier Colt. He snapped off a shot without pausing to take accurate aim.

An Apache fast approaching his right flank dropped his rifle and tumbled off his horse's back, hitting the ground headfirst and hard, breaking his neck. But the main body of war-painted riders had the edge over Jackson in speed and freshness and was undeterred by its comrade's fatal fall.

The hostiles fell in behind, bawling curses and threats; their fury doubled.

Jackson's sorrel mare was foam-drenched, its pace slipping. The Apaches drew alongside him, and when they realized his heavy, smoking six-gun was emptied, they cut in on him in a pincer movement.

With a flick of his wrist, Jackson twirled the gun in his hand, grabbing it by the barrel. Swerving his horse into the Indian nearest him, he brought the iron-framed butt hammering down on the man's skull, dodging the tomahawk that was raised equally offensively. The Indian expelled a breathy grunt. His eyeballs swivelled upwards and he slipped from the back of his mustang, going under its rear hoofs and bringing it down on top of him in a squealing, man-pulping crash.

While Jackson was downing the fellow, another redman scrambled on to his pony's back and took a flying leap at the scout, knocking him from the saddle.

Jackson hit clear ground in a controlled roll, but even so it was a bruising fall and took the breath out of him. Moreover, once on the ground, he was in danger of being trampled by the flying hoofs of his attackers' horses.

The Apaches wheeled and reined in. Fully a half-dozen jumped from their horses and piled on top of him, fighting mad.

Sat upon and pinned down, Jackson couldn't move. He was powerless to resist them. Sharp words from Angry-fist restrained the braves itching to bring their sharp knives and tomahawks to bear. As he'd envisaged, he wasn't to be allowed an easy end with no ceremony.

Quickly the Apaches bound his hands with leather thongs, and slung him over the back of his own snorting horse, regardless of its distress. They tied him there securely.

It was the most terrifying situation he'd known in his frontier life. He feared the death they planned for him would be slow, bloody and extremely painful.

Lilian Goodnight said with greater confidence than she felt, 'You daren't hold me in your jail, Skene. What charges do you have?'

A small knot of interested spectators had gathered on Silver Vein's main drag when the makeshift posse from Boorman's Wells had jogged in with its prisoner and come to a halt outside the sheriff's office. Misfit Lil was always a good topic for gossip and, under apparent arrest, maybe a better one than usual.

Skene carefully slid her from his saddle. He sneered.

'For starters, we'll charge yuh with assistin' a declared felon to escape custody.'

'Mr Farraday wasn't in custody, and how the hell will you prove I knew he was any felon?'

Skene's mouth worked but only wheezes emerged. He didn't have an answer, and Lil felt her spirits lift, but her optimism was premature.

The man whose arm she'd wounded, said, 'She shot me an' bloodied my arm. It's godawful sore. I won't be able to do a lick o' work for weeks. That's unlawful, for certain-sure.'

'Lead was flying every which way out there,' Lil replied swiftly. 'A lot of gunsmoke was adrift over a heap of confusion. How can you be sure it was a bullet of mine that hit you? Could've been anyone's.'

A third posseman, the bear-sized one with the gun-clubbed nose, said in a thick voice, 'She broke my nose. Eb'ryone saw that. It were assault.'

'It was self-defence,' Lil retorted. 'I was an innocent woman being attacked by a group of wild men without justification.'

She noted with a leap of hope that the onlookers now included Stewart Peabody, the fussy Silver Vein attorney who'd done work for her father in the past. He was always on the lookout for the chance to exact a new fee from the wealthy Flying G spread.

She addressed him directly. 'What do you think, Mr Peabody?'

Peabody was an expert at his hums and hahs. 'Well, it's my considered opinion that in the final analysis it would be for the circuit judge to decide, young lady.' He stroked his silver hair. 'Hmmm ... of course it would be! However, I could envisage a suit for wrongful arrest might well arise, and given that your parent, Mr Benjamin Goodnight, is an influential rancher and might be prevailed upon–'

'Hey! Don't let the bitch get away with anythin'!' a new contributor broke in.

Lil's spirits had been about to take off and truly soar when the intervener thrust his way to the front of the small crowd. He also had an arm in a sling, and was maliciously determined to swing the debate against Misfit Lil. The man was vengeful Cole Lansbury, the Silver Vein johnny-come-lately she'd provoked in McHendry's saloon the night the news had been brought of Angry-fist's breakout from the reservation.

Lansbury ploughed on. 'You want charges to hold the gal on, Sheriff, you can have gun-shootin' in enclosed premises and wounding with intent. She was drunk on private-stock

114

whiskey an' done broke my wrist without reason. I got all the witnesses needed. My friend, Frank Randolph, was right there and follered the business entire. She skedaddled real sharpish, knowin' she was in the wrong.'

'You asshole!' Lil said. 'Nohow was it like that!'

'That's enough!' Skene said hoarsely.

'It ain't half enough!'

But Skene said to Lansbury, 'Bully for you, citizen. Step right into my office and swear out the complaint, will yuh?'

Peabody did some more distracted hair-smoothing, looking gravely cogitative but saying nothing on the fresh development.

Skene took a firm grip on Lil and hustled her into his office.

'I bet he's got no busted wing,' she protested. 'It was just a flesh wound. Prob'ly a sore hole healing tight, is all.'

Off the street, Skene said sotto voce, but with a harsh and grating gloat, 'Yuh're a fine piece o' tight flesh your ownself, missy. An' in the cells of a dark night when the town's a-sleepin' yuh'll l'arn all about sore holes...'

'I doubt it! I'll fight you to the last, tooth and nail.'

'Yuh'll act nice, or I'll lock yuh in a cell with a passel o' drunk hardcases, an' give 'em the chance to take turns. Would yuh cotton to that?'

The laughter frothed stickily in his throat. 'Might do it anyways.'

Jackson Farraday's captors took him to a secret Apache place in the higher country. It was reached through a narrow, twisting defile beyond which a much broader area of tall Indian ricegrass gave way to a tiny green jewel of a foothill meadow, complete with a bubbling spring and stunted pines. In some ways, except for its seclusion, it resembled the meadow where Jackson had found his horse. Here the Indians' tough, small mustangs had green feed aplenty and the party had set up an encampment as a base for their raiding.

Jackson saw many tepees, a few of the traditional, painted buffalo skin, but others of tawdry canvas. Several womenfolk had joined the reservation jumpers. One woman, he noted, had had her nose amputated flat to her face. He knew it was the barbaric practice of the Apache people to mutilate the adulterous squaw in this way.

He began to see the glimmer of a chance that he might be able to appeal to these people's primitive sense of fair play and justice. Jackson's talents were wide and extraordinary. He'd long earned a living on the violent and uncivilized frontier, but he was an educated man who spoke seven languages and several Indian dialects. Maybe he could parley with Angry-fist.

But the rebels' showy leader, resplendent in war bonnet, moose-skin shirt and leggings fringed with ermine, stood well back and watched impassively. Jackson was dragged from his horse and tied to a sturdy pole in the middle of the encampment. For the rest of the day, he was left in the heat of the sun, the object of occasional ridicule or revilement.

At dusk, a fire was lit virtually at his feet. The younger braves circled round him to the beat of drums, screaming and stamping. Their smooth, bronze bodies glistened with oil and medicine paint. Some shook vicious spiked clubs; others brandished wickedly sharp scalping knives.

Beads of sweat soon stood on Jackson's brow in the flickering glow of the firelight.

Soon, a new game commenced. Arrows and tomahawks were thrown at him. Several buried their sharp heads in the pole to which he was tied. He knew the narrow misses were all part of the cruel psychology, if the Apaches' customs could be given that name. The braves were deliberately aiming their weapons wide as a contribution to the torture that would culminate in his violent, drawn-out and gory death.

A lull came in the Apaches' hideous hymn of chanted hate. Spotting Angry-fist drawing closer, no doubt to revel in his flinching, melting discomfort, or order the next stage in his slow demise, Jackson yelled out to him in his own tongue.

'Stop this madness, Angry-he-shakes-fist! I am not your enemy. Listen to my story. I, too, am now an outcast under the white man's laws.'

Intrigued, perhaps, by Jackson's facility with his tribal tongue, Angry-fist made a sign and the chanting died away altogether.

'Speak then, long-haired one, but do not lie, for you are in our power and we have seen you fighting Apaches in the company of the bluecoats.'

'I have long been the Apache's friend, loving the land even as he does, wanting to smell the sunlight and hear the trees grow.'

Angry-fist scowled like a surly child. 'This is idle talk to flatter and deceive. It is not the story you promised.'

'Untie me and give me water. My throat is

parched by sun and fire.'

Angry-fist scowled some more but rapped orders for Jackson to be taken from the pole. 'Cut him loose!'

He was so weak that when the Indians let go of him, he couldn't stand without support and slumped to the ground. But once he'd been given water, he began his story.

'The white men pursue me even as they do Angry-fist. I am accused of killing a white woman.' He looked around, gathering his strength and breath, and pointed to the Indian woman without a nose. 'She was one who had given offence like her – an adulteress.'

The Indians set to murmuring and Angry-fist said, 'But you did not cut off squaw's nose – you killed her. Is this the white man's way?'

'It is not. Nor did I kill her. Could be it was her lawful husband who did that – the man who runs the trading post at Boorman's Wells.'

Angry-fist glared. He was plainly unhappy. 'He who is called Axel Boorman is our friend. He sell us whiskey we cannot get on Fort Dennis reservation.'

'Is that so?' Jackson said, trying not to betray his own displeasure, though the trade in jars of rotgut was no deep secret. Corn was plentiful and the distillation process simple, making the *aqua vitae* cheap and easy to manufacture. The chief danger to the consumer of moonshine whiskey was the fusel oil content. Germs were sure to be killed by the alcohol.

Then Angry-fist dropped his bombshell. 'The white trader Boorman also promise to sell us newest army rifles, so we no longer need bows and arrows and old flintlocks.'

Jackson was flabbergasted and, forgetting the whiskey, he could for a moment only gulp.

'I don't believe it,' he muttered at last. 'How can you buy such rifles?'

'With many dollars. Boorman tell us how and where to get the white-man's foolish treasure in such quantity.'

'By robbing the army pay wagon!' Jackson exclaimed, instantly recalling the grisly fate of Major Pelham and his escort which had held the beginnings of his own downfall. 'That explains something at last. I guess I was wrong. You do speak the truth, Angry-fist.'

His mind was racing. Boorman a gun-runner! This startling information had to be passed to the military immediately. Possibly his own reputation could be restored. But would he be believed?

Or must he first chance his arm and return to Boorman's Wells and find the whereabouts of a damning cache of hidden rifles that the trading post owner was offering to the renegade Indians?

Though he was figuratively back on his feet – almost – he was still far from free to go. If Angry-fist guessed at his intentions, his feet were sure to be quickly kicked out from under him again.

10

TOMAHAWK DUEL

Jackson Farraday made nothing more of the promised guns.

'Brothers,' he began in a conciliatory tone, 'I will help you walk once more the path of peace. I will go to the bluecoats' chief at Fort Dennis and plead your case and your grievances, lest you be seen guilty of treason and insurrection.'

Angry-fist made a high, trilling noise that Jackson took to be ridicule or mirth. It was echoed by the closest of his followers.

'We do not want your help, Longhair. We do not trust the bluecoats, especially not the hateful one they call Covington.'

'Lieutenant Covington is young and rash, but the fort's commanding officer is Colonel Lexborough, an older man, fair and honest. He will speak with the Peace Commission. If you are granted amnesty, you may rely on him completely.'

Jackson thought he might be getting somewhere. Angry-fist was weighing his words. But the Apache finished his pondering with a contemptuous, dismissive gesture, drawing attention to Jackson's plight.

'Look! You are in my power and have no chance to speak to your Lexborough.'

Jackson knew he couldn't deny it, or give up. 'Let us parley some more, Angry-fist. To find it worthwhile for us both that I regain my freedom.'

'I have no need of your pow-wow with Lexborough. In their hearts, my people have never surrendered to the white man. Now we show off our strength to other Apaches,' Angry-fist said flatly, but one of his band, an older man, approached him and spoke in a whisper, making him chuckle.

Jackson wondered what the hell was going on.

Angry-fist raised his head imperiously and said, 'Very well. I have listened and we will make a bargain, Longhair. We will give you one chance. You will be matched against myself in single combat. It will be, as the white-eyes call it, a sport. Win and we spare you to leave. Lose and you die!'

Jackson knew from experience that many of the Indian tribes respected men who could outfight them, but this proposal was putting the struggle on a personal level. He could appreciate how victory for Angry-fist over a man who'd bested several of the misguided youngsters who'd followed him would boost his status among the rebel band and the Apaches in general.

'Very well. I accept your chance,' Jackson said. It was out of the question to show a loss of nerve.

Angry-fist was confident to the point of arrogance. 'You are a fool, but at least you are brave. When the spirit departs your worthless carcass, they will say Angry-fist has become possessed of its courage in this world. It will be seen by everyone that he is all-powerful.'

The combat planned was a duel with tomahawks. They were to be lashed together by their left wrists. Each antagonist would be armed with a tomahawk in the right hand. A buzz of anticipation fell to a hush as the preparations were completed.

Angry-fist, divested of the showy war bonnet and other trappings, his body gleaming with medicine paint and oil, called upon the Apache god.

'Yosen, be with me!'

Then he took the first, sweeping swing with his tomahawk.

Jackson ducked and stepped back, dragging his opponent with him. The sharp blades clashed ringingly as Jackson used his to fend off the blow.

Angry-fist growled and pulled Jackson toward him, raising his tomahawk for a second swing, but affording the white scout a chance to strike back.

Jackson blinked sweat out of his eyes and took it. Quick on his feet, the Indian danced aside and Jackson's weapon glanced off his oiled thigh, leaving not a scratch visible.

Flourishes and counter-flourishes were parried in quick succession. No blood was drawn by the scary, whirling blades, but Jackson was alarmed to feel his control over his tomahawk was affected by the several blows it had sustained from Angry-fist's. No, it wasn't his imagination – the head of the tomahawk was working loose, and its unreliable balance was consistently spoiling his aim.

Jackson suspected trickery; that the wily Apaches had equipped him with a dud weapon for the duel.

His fear was confirmed when, two more lunges and lurches later, the head of his tomahawk parted from the haft. The metal went hurtling end over end high in the air, leaving him with just a stick of lumber to defend himself.

The Apaches shrieked with glee. Angry-fist's lips drew back from his teeth in a hideous grin. Victory was his.

'You die, Longhair!'

But Jackson was warned of and ready for the loss. He'd realized already the hopelessness of continuing the contest, man to man, face to face on foot, without a matching weapon.

'So it ain't gonna be a fair fight, huh?'

He promptly swooped under Angry-fist's guard, whacking his shins with the wooden handle and toppling the pair of them to the ground.

'Down you go, you mangy bastard!'

They rolled and grappled in the dust, their left wrists still attached.

A fight to the death, it was no time or place for gentlemanly fair play. Jackson let go of the tomahawk handle, useless at close quarters, and seized Angry-fist's right wrist. They strained and writhed, but Angry-fist didn't perceive Jackson's tactic till it was too late and Farraday's teeth locked themselves in his forearm.

Jackson bit down mightily on the slippery, oiled flesh. He felt his teeth go through the skin; tasted the escape of the Indian's salty blood into his mouth, mingled with the foulness of medicine oil. He dared not let up to spit it out.

'*Aiieee!*'

Angry-fist screamed in rage and pain. Involuntarily, he released his grip on his tomahawk. The instant it span to the ground to one side of them, both men broke off every other striving, every hold, to pounce for it.

Desperate, but knowing exactly what he had sought to accomplish, Jackson's hand reached the tomahawk first. He scooped it up, clenching and swinging all in one continuous movement.

With a meaty thud, the keen head chopped through Angry-fist's left forearm just above the leather thong that linked them together.

Angry-fist screamed again. This time it was a piercing shriek that turned the blood of the most impassive of the witnessing Apaches to ice-water. His eyes glazed in impotent horror as he watched the blood spurt in a fountain from his wrist.

Jackson jerked away, clutching the blood-stained tomahawk in his right hand and with Angry-fist's severed hand dangling from his left wrist. Letting out a terrifying roar of his own, he ran at the circle of Apaches, swinging the tomahawk.

They were startled by the sudden turn of events; shocked at the vanquishing of their leader. They parted like a line of trees struck by a tornado, and Jackson stormed through to where the Indians' ponies and his sorrel mare were tethered.

He didn't pause to find his missing rig. He cut the tether, swung on to the horse's bare back and dug in his heels. Behind him, the renegade Apaches were yelling and running for their own mounts, and he knew he had to work hurriedly if he was to make good his escape.

Shrill whoops rent the twilight letting him know the chase was on in earnest. The affronted Apaches were more bent than ever on taking his scalp.

He soon reached the area of golden Indian rice-grass. The erect bunches were profuse, growing some two-and-a-half feet tall. The expanse was also dry as tinder from the summer drought. Once the sorrel had passed through, Jackson made a brief halt. He took a box of phosphorous matches from a pocket in his broadcloth pants and struck one. After he'd waited for it to ignite properly, he tossed it back into the dry rice-grass.

Only the one, first match was needed. In a

flash, the brittle growth caught alight. The flames were fanned by a steady, canyon-lands breeze, and spread with satisfying strength and speed, leaping back toward the Apache encampment.

All pursuit by the Indians was curtailed. Jackson wondered that they'd never been aware of the vulnerability of their camp in the event of such a grass fire. In this direction, the hidden place was effectively cut off by his quick-thinking action.

Through the clouds of billowing, acrid smoke, he glimpsed Apache riders struggling to control their terrified ponies as they turned to flee and save themselves. Squeals of animals and cries of men, both in blind panic, were succeeded by a retreating rumble of hoofs that could denote only a mad stampede for safety back up the valley.

The challenge for Jackson was now survival. He was slumped almost double, his nose close to the sorrel's mane. He rode into the night, letting the sorrel proceed at an even walk. Above him, a white moon rose in a sky dusted with bright specks of starlight. Hunger, returning thirst and exhaustion were his companions. These plus restlessness – a sense of urgent things remaining to be done.

What had happened to the girl, Misfit Lil, who'd taken pains to help him when everyone else had seemingly turned against him? Where was she now?

What would happen to himself, should he show up in Silver Vein or Boorman's Wells?

His tired brain ranged feverishly over the startling information he'd acquired of Boorman's perfidy. He would need proof, of course. If he levelled accusations without it, they would be seen as a kind of tit-for-tat desperation. Boorman, backed by the corrupt Silver Vein sheriff, Willard Skene, had fitted him out for a necktie party as the killer of Esther Boorman. His name was blackened. Any wild story about Boorman gunrunning to hostile Apaches would be seen in this unsympathetic light.

He came gradually to a resolve to ride first to Fort Dennis where he might be afforded at least a neutral reception. As he'd told Angry-fist, the fort's commander, Colonel Lexborough, was a good and fair man. He could advise him of what he'd heard, and have some hope of being allowed to go seek out the damning cache of rifles he reckoned he'd find hidden somewhere in Boorman's Wells.

Colonel Lexborough would be aware that

rumours had long been rife in army circles of organized thefts of weaponry and ammunition from government warehouses and freight shipments. The ring responsible allegedly had contacts all along the rugged trails from Montana to Mexico. Through these, the thieves disposed of their dangerous but valuable loot. Hostile bands of Indians would be reckoned suitable customers by the unscrupulous organizers of the racket.

Small traders in isolated places, like Axel Boorman, would be used as vital last links in the secret chain of supply and disposal. They would no doubt be rewarded with a healthy cut of the profits from the dirty business.

Here, maybe, was where Wheezer Skene fitted in. He had a nose for smelling out and cutting himself into any money-making venture in the territory, be it fair or foul.

Jackson reflected soberly that the scandalous case could make or break him. Succeed, and his reputation as one of the army's top civilian scouts would be restored; fail, and a hangrope awaited him.

But his present wretched physical state precluded a direct ride to the old military wagon road and on to Fort Dennis. More by instinct than conscious skill, he directed his horse to a spring-watered stopping place known to them both and where he could rest up awhile.

In the shelter of this bottom, where a level patch of green was shaded by willows and cottonwoods, he turned his attention to the gruesome dead hand dangling by a tight leather thong from his left wrist.

He cut through the thong and threw the disgusting object as far from him as he could manage.

He shuddered. 'Ugh! There'll be no more angry fists made with that piece of carrion!'

11

'THROW HIM IN
THE BLACK HOLE!'

The jailhouse in Silver Vein where Misfit Lil was incarcerated was constructed along conventional lines from Utah granite quarried from Little Cottonwood Canyon in Salt Lake County. The calaboose was three cells in a row, adjoining the sheriff's office and fronted with heavy-barred, floor-to-ceiling grille doors. Each cell had a small barred window set into the thick stone at the rear; each had a solid but battered wooden bunk and a palliasse stacked with blankets of nondescript colour and doubtful cleanliness.

The hard, echo-producing stone was responsible for interesting acoustics. Leastways, Misfit Lil thought they were interesting. By keeping her ears cocked, she reckoned she might learn much about the shenanigans Sheriff Willard Skene hid behind his tin star.

Skene and Boorman had accepted that Jackson Farraday was lying dead back in an inaccessible canyon, where his broken body would be picked to pieces by the buzzards, the coyotes and other varmints. Naturally, Lil found this upsetting. She couldn't really believe it, and didn't know why – till she observed an army of ants climbing up and down, in and around a crevice between the stone blocks in one corner of her cell. It reminded her of something buried deep in her extensive knowledge of this wild expanse of country she called home.

The vertical wall of the canyon below the amphitheatre from where Jackson was said to have plunged to his death contained a fissure, said by the Indians to be negotiable by a strong and nimble climber. Adventurous though she was, she'd never tried it herself – had, in fact, forgotten it – but the toing and froing of the persistent ants in their crack brought the picture back to her mind.

Had Jackson known about the fissure? Had he succeeded in finding and using it? Her hopes sparked optimistically and became a blaze. She convinced herself Jackson had escaped and lived.

Axel Boorman, too, was niggled by doubts that the frontiersman they'd accused of his wife's murder was dead.

'Don't matter if he ain't so,' Skene snapped back at him. 'Didn't yuh say he'd given Esther a ring? We'll say they were havin' an affair. They argued an' she refused to give it back, so he killed her. It'll sound good as a motive – in court or out – an' the ring's evidence.'

Boorman reached in his vest pocket for a cigar and bit off the end before lighting it. 'Sure, I got the ring,' he said between puffs. 'I guess it'd damn Jackson Farraday. It's engraved with a letter "J". Shows he was back of something with my wife.'

'Yuh don't say,' Skene said, in a slightly stricken voice that might have been produced other than by asthma. 'Waal, if he does show up, we prob'ly won't need the ring anyways. Fact is, women killers ain't popular hereabouts. Folks've been lynched for less. I'll fix it so's he won't have a prayer – or a hope in hell.'

The thought gladdened Skene and he essayed a rasping laugh to convince Boorman of his momentarily shaken confidence.

The two men were oblivious or uncaring that Lil was eavesdropping on their conversation, hoping to hear something shady she could use against them.

What their words divulged to her, coupled with knowledge she already had, exceeded her every expectation.

Jackson Farraday was on foot, leading his saddle-less horse. He was hatless, his clothing was ripped and scorched. He was dust-grimed and smoke-stained. His chin-beard was untrimmed and there was stubble on his face.

Above him, the sun was heading inexorably toward its zenith. Though he utilized what little shadow was still provided by the sorrel mare, the heat pressed down on his shoulders and bent back like a heavy load. But the plain he travelled on was hospitable country after what he'd been through, and in the distance loomed the reassuring bulk of Fort Dennis. The south side of the main building and its plank roof were visible behind the solid lumber gates in the stockade fence. The flag flew over the garrison.

The fierce, mid-morning sun glinted off field-glasses. He figured he'd been observed.

He must cut a bizarre and sorry figure in the eyes of the watching sentries patrolling the high catwalk inside the stockade. He wondered if he'd been recognized and what kind of a reception he would get. He was

136

sick himself of the stink of the dried sweat on his skin and in his filthy duds.

When he reached the fort's great wooden gates, they swung open to admit him.

'Jackson Farraday, and I request to see Colonel Lexborough,' he said.

The sentry snapped to attention, though Jackson thought he detected a repressed grin on his face, like he was amused by his appearance... or he knew something he (Jackson) didn't. 'Very good, Mr Farraday sir, an orderly will escort you to the – er – colonel's office.'

They went across the broad, level parade-ground to the stone-built administration building. Jackson felt at home in the sur-roundings. He heard the familiar sounds of muffled commands, the neighing of horses, the clang of a hammer on an anvil. Fort Dennis was a mixture of log blockhouses, housing the men's barracks, the stables, the blacksmith's shop and the mess shack, and stone structures. The latter included officers' quarters, the infirmary, a commissary and the guardhouse – all evidence to the avail-ability of rock nearby and the masons to shape it.

'Wait here,' the orderly said when they'd reached the spartan corridor outside the fort commandant's office.

Jackson began to relax. He was conscious his appearance didn't come up to spick and span army standards, but no matter – Colonel Lexborough was a rugged, seasoned type of mature years and would understand when he received his report.

But moments later, when he was ushered into the office, his stomach fell to his battered boots. The man who sat behind the paper-strewn desk wasn't the distinguished, grey-haired colonel: it was Lieutenant Michael Covington.

'You!' Jackson croaked, conveying his disappointment without thinking. 'What are you doing in here?'

'I'm in command. Colonel Lexborough is on furlough in Salt Lake City with his good lady, and your impertinent question is exactly the one I should be asking you!'

'No need to be officious, Lieutenant,' Farraday said evenly, trying to make allowances for the younger man's prickliness. 'I've come to tell you where Angry-fist's renegades are holed up. I had a run-in with the crazy Injun. It was costly for him – I had to hack off his left hand.'

Covington was unimpressed, or disbelieving.

'Your presence here amounts to trespass, Mr Farraday,' he said. 'You were banished from the fort when I dismissed you from its payroll. Furthermore, I understand you're wanted for murder by the civilian authorities.'

In his weary and filthy state, Jackson found it hard to be respectful to the smartly uniformed popinjay.

'Do I take it the army here has lost interest in the reservation jumpers?' he growled. 'I've ridden here straight away at no small inconvenience to make a report.'

'You're a wanted criminal and your word is therefore suspect. Your tale is as wild as any told by your accomplice.'

'Who do you mean? Misfit Lil?'

'Yes, Mr Farraday, that Goodnight girl who had you fooled in the badlands, and who is now apparently held in the Silver Vein jail for trial.'

'Good God! If Skene harms her, he'll have that to answer for, too. I know she can be a damn nuisance, but hasn't anyone spoken up for her? Raised bail?'

Covington looked at Jackson distastefully. 'She's a wilful, mean-mouthed brat who gives people nothing but headaches and trouble. Her credibility *here* is at zero.'

'And what about my credibility? Aren't you going to dispatch men to mop up Angry-fist and his band?'

'What proof do I have of your story?' Covington's nose twitched. 'Where is this – amputated hand?'

'Hell, boy, I came to lend a live hand, not bring a bloody souvenir!'

Jackson stormed to a territorial map on the office wall. His eyes flashed angrily.

'Your Apache war party is here,' he said, jabbing a finger at the canyonlands and leaving a dirty print. 'I left 'em kinda burned out. I'd advise you send a column of cavalry before they recover. As for me, I've had enough of playing soldiers with you. I'm riding on!'

Covington stepped round the big desk and barred Jackson's way.

'Not so fast, Mr Farraday. You'll remain here, in the guardhouse. Sheriff Willard Skene will be informed of your detention.'

Jackson was amazed. 'Have you lost your senses, Covington? I never killed Esther Boorman.'

'A court will decide on that, no doubt. First, I'll seek direction from my superiors. As I see it, it will be the sheriff's responsibility to arrest you, prefer charges and shift you to the appropriate accommodation, which I'll suggest is in the Silver Vein jail, along with your juvenile friend, Miss Goodnight.'

Jackson played what he reckoned was his trump card. 'Now see here, you still don't know the half of it. I reckon Skene is in cahoots with Axel Boorman and I'm being framed. Boorman is gunrunning to the Apaches.'

Covington's jaw dropped, but he blustered on. 'So you are as stupid as your female sidekick! Having murdered your accuser's wife, you now seek to blacken his name with the most far-fetched hogwash I've ever heard.'

'I'm standing no more of this. Let me outa here, you fool! You can be damn sure I aim to find all the evidence you or anyone will need. That and get Lil outa Skene's rotten jail.'

'You'll stay put, Mr Farraday!' Covington snapped.

'The hell with that, you pompous asshole!'

When Jackson made to go past him to the door, Covington moved swiftly to block his path more completely. Jackson pushed at him roughly.

'Keep your hands off me, you dirty ruffian!' Covington said. He took a step back and swung a retaliatory fist at Jackson's face.

Covington could teach Jackson nothing about how to conduct himself in fisticuffs. The blow hit, but only glancingly. Jackson had instantly and almost instinctively shifted his head away from it.

The fight was on. Jackson feinted with his right, slammed home a left to Covington's heart, a right to his chin, another left to his body.

Covington backed up and the pair found themselves standing toe to toe in the middle of the office, slugging it out. But Jackson's ordeals of the past thirty-six hours had left him weakened, and the young lieutenant was fresh and filled with indignation at having his authority challenged.

Jackson took a series of jolting punches to the body that winded him. For a split second his guard was down. Covington caught him on the right temple with a cracking blow that dimmed his senses and made him reel dizzily. He tripped over his own feet and crashed to the floor.

Covington opened the door. 'Sergeant! Some men here, at the double. Take Mr Farraday to the guardhouse cells – throw him in the black hole!'

The soldiers' hands that fastened on Jackson weren't gentle. To them, he was a woman-killer. His disgusting appearance and smell backed every unsavoury smear they'd heard.

Jackson was hauled to his feet and dragged away. Multiple leering faces filled his blurred vision. He tried to pull free; he kicked. Distantly, he heard laughter, muffled as though his head was under water.

He struggled some more, mightily.

His blue-coated captors lost patience with him. He was pummelled unmercifully, till he retched on his empty stomach.

Once he was powerless to resist further, he was hauled back across the parade-ground to the guardhouse.

The interior of the stone building was divided in two sections. The front section functioned as the headquarters for the men on guard duty. It was a centre of activity in the fort, manned twenty-four hours a day. From here, the soldiers took turns with sentry duty, guarding the entrance and manning the catwalk – the continuous platform inside the four walls of the stockade, easily reached by ladders at strategic positions. The section was furnished with gun racks, fire buckets and cots where soldiers might rest during breaks in their spells of duty.

The second section of the Fort Dennis guardhouse served as a prison for soldiers convicted of military crimes or awaiting court-martial trials. It had two main cells and a so-called 'black hole', or solitary confinement cell.

Jackson's attackers carried him into the jail. His body ached, his mouth was torn and bleeding, his eyes had partially closed. But he knew where he was and heard the dry hinges of a heavy door groan.

He was thrown forward helplessly and in agony. He rolled down a short flight of steps and struck his head on cold flagstones at the bottom.

He was in the black hole. That was what registered before oblivion swallowed him up.

12

JAILBREAK

The ants were still patrolling the wall of Misfit Lil's cell. She'd also discovered other small wildlife in the fusty blankets and straw-filled palliasse on the bunk. But it could be worse, she figured.

Sheriff Willard Skene hadn't tried to molest her the first night. Nor, as far as she knew, had he made any attempt to contact her father at the Flying G ranch. A free spirit, release into her pa's unforgiving custody was one of the last things she wanted to happen. His air of long-suffering and indignation did nothing for a girl's selfrespect.

She'd had time to come to terms with her fear of Skene's unwanted attentions. She'd brushed him off before, successfully, and she reckoned she was even more in command of her emotions now – tougher, stronger. Jail was also better than death.

What had happened to Jackson Farraday? She was still alive, wasn't beaten yet, still had a fighting chance of regaining freedom. Thankfully, she was largely uninjured except for a quickly healing scratched arm from the gunfight with the posse.

News of Jackson came to her like everything else in this minor hell-hole. She overheard goings-on in the sheriff's office.

Late in the day, an excited deputy brought a report to Skene. Four talkative soldiers playing cards in McHendry's saloon had let drop that Farraday, after being seized by the military at Fort Dennis, was in custody in the post's guardhouse. Lieutenant Mike Covington, acting in Colonel Lexborough's absence, was requesting direction from higher command.

'Damnation! So the bastard did git out of the badlands,' Skene said. 'Waal, his charmed life ain't gonna last, I'll see to that. I'll be over to the fort first light. He has to be held here, to stand trial for the murder of Esther Boorman. Yuh c'n spread the word that by tomorrer night he's gonna be sittin' pretty in this here jail. He'll be waitin' fer what's comin' to him, yuh savvy?'

The deputy nodded. 'I need no pictures painted, boss. The least time he has to wait, the better, right?'

'Yeah ... we c'n do without the botheration

of a court hearin'. It's one of those kinda open-and-shut cases, ain't it? 'Sides, the boys in town ain't had the chance of a good hangin' in a long while.'

Misfit Lil was horrified by Skene's bland tone. The suggestion that Jackson Farraday would be handed over to a lynch mob, virtually incited on Skene's orders, sickened her.

She had to get out of here, urgently. She'd have to go to Mike Covington at Fort Dennis and tell the poor sap what he'd be letting Jackson in for if he released him into the sheriff's hands.

How could she manage it? She'd been trying to dream up schemes of escape since the cell door had clanged shut on her. Maybe, in exchange for freedom, she could offer her body to Skene. That was what he'd said he wanted...

She dismissed the notion from consideration. It would be too much of a turnabout. Skene was nobody's fool. He was self-centred in his ambitions and opinions, but he'd scarcely believe she suddenly found him desirable, or was that anxious to be released. Moreover, she couldn't afford to gamble on him letting her go afterwards anyway.

Sweet talk was out: aggressive action was

in. She settled on the wildest of the half-baked plans she'd previously entertained but rejected as too risky. Now was the time for desperate measures.

She felt in an inner pocket of her buckskin jacket that her captors had failed to find when they'd searched her for weapons. What she had was a slim pack of phosphorous matches.

She went to her bunk and sat in the very corner on the straw mattress. She heaped the stinking blankets around her as though she was settling to sleep. Hidden beneath them, she began working at the half-rotten ticking on the palliasse. Soon, straw was poking through the hole she'd picked with her fingernails. She ripped at the hole and more spilled out with a rustle.

The blankets still shrouding her, she crouched over the pile of dirty straw and took out her matches. She figured she could ignite a fine little fire, hopefully with clouds of choking smoke but enough flames to throw a fright into Skene, forcing him to come into the cell.

Her first match wouldn't strike; the white head broke off. But she was luckier with the second and didn't have to nurse the blaze too much before it spread to the bug-infested blankets.

Lil was driven back, coughing, as the flames grew bigger. The smoke wreathed around her. Her eyes watered. She shouted; she screamed.

Skene jumped up from his desk, where he'd been reading a week-old copy of the *Salt Lake Tribune*. He cussed a blue streak. By the time he'd grabbed his bunch of keys, the smoke was swirling into his office.

Misfit Lil realized she should have saved her breath instead of having to replace it with the choking smoke. Fixing her neckerchief over her lower face, she dropped to her hands and knees where the air was clearer, but also foxing that she was senseless.

'What in hell's name yuh done, gal?' Skene snarled. 'Yuh wanna git yuhself killed?'

Lil thought the answers to both his questions were obvious. Under the neckerchief her lips twitched in a crooked, devil-may-care smile.

Wheezing as the smoke affected him, Skene unlocked and opened the cell door and strode in to grab her.

The minute his hand fastened on her collar, Lil leaped up. She kicked him hard in the shins. Her mouth was a tight, thin line, but her watering eyes still glittered with malicious pleasure.

He hopped, grunting. 'Why, you dirty li'l–'

She chopped at the back of his thick neck with a hard-edged hand. The force of the jarring blow shot up her still-sore arm; she gritted her teeth, stifling a gasp.

Dazed, he stumbled forward and she propelled him with a kick to his backside into the smoky cell. Then she was out, slamming the iron-barred cell door and turning the key he'd left conveniently in the lock.

The loud click revived Skene's reeling senses. 'Hey!' he blurted with rasping urgency. 'Yuh can't leave me in here – I'll suffocate!'

Lil scoffed. 'You've got me mixed up with someone who gives a shit.'

She didn't think the asthmatic sheriff would choke, let alone burn to death, but too bad if he did. This was more than a bit of mischief she was playing – like it or not, Misfit Lil was having to live up to her reputation for being a real hardcase.

How else could you deal with a liar who was ready to commission a murder to cover up another murder?

It seemed to her that Axel Boorman was the likeliest suspect as the killer of his wife, Esther. What she couldn't understand was why Skene, whose main interests in life were collecting money and satisfying his own appetites, should be protecting the trading-post operator and setting up Jackson Farraday to take the rap.

She stopped only to throw down Skene's keys on his scarred desk and to recover her confiscated gun rig from the cupboard where she'd seen Skene cast it. She buckled the belt around her hips on the run.

What she needed next was a horse that would take her to Fort Dennis before the disturbance at the jailhouse came to the town's attention and she was on the dodge from the inevitable hue and cry.

A row of saddled horses stood at the hitch rail outside McHendry's. One had a Flying G brand on its left flank, and she was passingly familiar with its abilities and habits. She untethered the horse and jumped astride.

'Giddap!' she cried and pounded out of Silver Vein beneath a cloud of dust.

Misfit Lil arrived at the fort entrance just as the sun was dipping toward the horizon of the vast treeless plain to the west, painting the table-flat land a fiery gold.

The sentries let her in, but were puzzled. She could imagine them asking one another,

'What does the fool gal want here? Hasn't she caused us enough trouble already?'

She slipped from the horse's back. 'I have to see Mike Covington fast,' she announced. 'It's an emergency.'

An elderly sergeant said, 'It's *Lieutenant* Covington, missy, and we'll have to see about that. I'll send an orderly–'

'Don't worry,' she said, dodging past him lithely. 'I know the way.'

Under her breath, as she ran toward the administration block, she added, 'The old dodderer! He can't give me the runaround.'

Lil had an unerring knack for finding her way about even places she'd visited only occasionally. She went directly to Colonel Lexborough's office, where she correctly guessed she'd find Covington sitting in for his absent chief.

Covington wasn't happy when she came into the office, especially since she caught him reading what looked like a dime novel which he quickly covered with a pile of duty rosters.

'Miss Goodnight!' he exclaimed. 'What are you doing, bursting in here without a word of lea–?'

'Michael Covington, if you think I can wait for your boys to roll out the red carpet, you're making a big mistake! This is urgent.'

'Then follow good manners and the proper procedure!'

'Procedure ... aaargh! You're making me mad!'

'You *always* make me mad, you wilful, cocksure bitch!'

'Now who's forgetting his manners? I don't like that kind of talk. But let's change the subject, shall we? You've got to release Jackson Farraday.'

Covington let his eyes roll in exasperated disbelief. 'So that's what this is about! I heard of your foolishness in aiding the man. Clearly, he's run amok ... murdering, making wild reports.'

'You utter fool, Mike! I lay my life Jackson Farraday is innocent of every charge laid against him.'

'You're out of line, young lady! And aren't you supposed to be in Sheriff Skene's jail?'

'Skene is a crook!' she flared. 'He's shielding the real culprit. I know Mr Farraday didn't shoot Esther Boorman. He'd quit the Wells before the shot was fired. And another thing, there's a–'

Covington jumped to his feet, waving his hands. 'Enough! If the charge is trumped up, let him exonerate himself when the case comes to trial.'

'Oh, you're impossible!' Lil spat out. 'I was going to tell you about the ring, but I'd be plumb wasting my time. There's going to be no trial. Skene is planning a necktie party for Jackson. If you hand him over, he'll be lynched!'

A tentative knocking came at the door. 'Are you all right in there, sir?'

Turning to the door, Lil promptly called out, 'Of course he's all right. Why don't you mind your own business?'

Covington reddened. 'Return to your duties, Sergeant! I don't need a nursemaid to deal with a silly child.'

What might have been an insubordinate harrumph from the corridor was followed by the plod of retreating footfalls.

'On second thoughts,' Lil said, 'maybe you should have ordered him to go free Mr Farraday from the guardhouse. I know you're a decent lad at bottom.'

Covington spluttered. 'Look here, girl, Farraday stays right where he is! You don't give me orders. Nor will you cajole me with female wiles.'

'Huh! What kind of girl do you think I am? You'd be the last man I'd show wiles.'

'I wouldn't want to see them, you crazy

frontier brat! You're a skinny thing, a scrawny pullet, a bony, flat-bosomed nubbin–'

Lil said, 'Don't you talk to me like that! Who do you think you are? Name-calling ain't apt to be reckoned polite, Michael Covington. Surely *you* know that. And it don't help getting mad.'

'I'm not mad!'

'But you just said you were. And anyway, I am.'

In fact, she was infuriated that her presence always so readily reduced him to confusion.

'You're so stupid you'd make anyone mad. To be exact, you're a bigger idiot than I knew if you're not going to free Jackson.'

Covington sighed. 'Look, don't let me tell you again. I'm sorry if–'

'Sorry don't get it done! What's more, it makes you a stinker!'

'Get out, Goodnight!'

'I'm wasting my words,' Lil said. 'Good night to you, too.'

Her pleas had failed. She left, slamming the door in final contempt.

13

QUICK WITS, QUICK LIME

Misfit Lil was determined not to leave Fort Dennis without Jackson Farraday. It was crucial to his life, to her continued freedom, and to confounding whatever foul scheme was afoot between Willard Skene and Axel Boorman.

Speed was of the essence. Mike Covington had proved he was an idiot. She had to overlook the obstacles, forget the dangers and come up with something fast that would allow her to release Jackson from the guardhouse's black hole herself.

When she left Colonel Lexborough's office, she didn't leave the administration building but went swiftly along the corridor to a walkway that gave access to the officers' quarters. Between these and the commissary were located privies of three kinds: for officers, for men and for women. Although there were no female soldiers, allowance was made at the fort for a percentage of the muster-roll to be married women.

Although the men's privies had no seats, the officers' and women's did. Lil turned into the women's privies and took a seat. She had to think – hard.

To release Jackson, she'd have first to clear the guardhouse. Somehow...

The feat seemed to be beyond even Misfit Lil's resources. Then it came to her. She was sitting on a possible answer!

She knew the privies were flushed out using the fort's drainage system. Rain and waste water collected from grates on the parade-ground was held behind a sluice gate. Periodically, the gate was opened and the water would flush the privy waste away into an old, underground streambed from which the fresh water had been diverted by pumps at a higher level for the fort's use.

Lil was so startled by the brilliance of her plan that she went cold and her nerve-ends tingled.

'Jeez,' she breathed, 'it all fits together dandy – just like the picture on one of them newfangled jigsaw puzzles with the cut-up hardwood pieces.'

If she blocked the exit from the gully under the privies, then opened the sluice gates, a flood would result. And the water would spill into the neighbouring commissary storehouse.

Now as well as the boxes of hardtack, the barrels of salt pork and the sacks of potatoes – the beans, the clothing and the tools – Fort Dennis's commissary housed lime; many heavy casks of it were in constant stock in the basement.

Lime was used for making mortar, plaster and whitewash. The mortar bound stones or bricks together in buildings' walls and filled the chinks between the logs of the more primitive blockhouses. The plaster was placed over wooden lathes to give a finer finish to walls and ceilings in the administration buildings and the superior officers' quarters. The whitewash was applied to the interior surfaces of the log structures.

So there was much call for the stuff around the place, but it had to be stored unslaked. The dryness was vital. Wet, or 'quick', it was nasty, corrosive material, causing severe burns, and Lil knew you had to wear gloves to handle it, and keep it from your eyes.

Also, while at the academy in Boston, she'd heard the dreadful story told by Virginia Bottomley, a girl from Maine whose father had been a ship's master.

Carrying a cargo of lime was always

fraught with peril. Moisture had gotten into the hold of Captain Bottomley's schooner's hold, and a chemical reaction had occurred, giving off great heat and increasing the lime hugely in volume.

The upshot was that the swelling lime had burst the casks and the ship had caught fire. Captain Bottomley and his vessel had been lost.

What Lil remembered from Virginia's story was lime had the enormous drawback that if the slightest amount of water reached the lime in the casks, it could catch on fire, and the fire was often inextinguishable.

Virginia had excused her father's failure to detect the looming tragedy that had befallen him. 'Poor Papa and most of his crew had head colds at the time. A ship's master needs a keen sense of smell in such situations. The odour of lime being slaked by water is an ominous danger signal...'

Apparently when a captain received such warning, every crack and crevice through which air might get into his vessel's hold – the doors and the portholes – was quickly to be sealed with plaster made from the quick-lime. Then the ship was headed for the nearest harbour and anchored a safe distance from shore and all other craft. For at any time it might burst into flames.

Lil hoped soldiers were as familiar as sailors with this frightening knowledge, for the success of her plan depended on it.

Blocking the privies' gully was no big problem. A quick dash from the women's room to the back of the blacksmith shop yielded Lil a sack of charcoal. She returned unchallenged and let it fall down the drop from the end privy. Partly filled, the sack was of just the right size, weight, softness and flexibility to lodge solidly in the channel running under it.

The next part was to open the sluice gate that would release the reservoir of undrinkable water used to flush the drains. Dusk had turned to night and, except for those doing sentry duty on the catwalk and in the guardhouse, most of the men were in their cots. Taps had sounded some time ago, signalling for lights to be put out in the soldiers' quarters. Nobody seemed to have taken a jot of notice of her Flying G horse, which had wandered over to a hitching place outside the stables.

Evidently the only threat the garrison could conceive of was a lightning raid by Angry-fist and his bunch of renegades, should they be so daring. All attention was turned outward for such an aggravation, minor though it would probably prove.

'Sloppy, Mike,' Misfit Lil tutted to herself with a chuckle. 'What would Colonel Lexborough say?'

Really, she did have the happiest knack of discomposing the young lieutenant and ruining his efficiency. This fort wasn't running well at all – and she intended to make matters far, far worse.

The short shaft down which the sluice gate was located was covered by a structure similar to a well's head. The gate was an iron plate which slid in grooves in the side of the shaft and was raised by a windlass. Once the gate was lifted, and water was rushing under it, replacing the gate was impossible until the pressure behind it was reduced almost to nothing. It was normal to raise the gate fairly cautiously – Misfit Lil had seen it done just once – but she intended to wind it up as rapidly as possible before she could be interrupted.

She was about to scoot across the parade-ground to the sluice gate head when two men, who'd been working late in the commissary, came out and headed for their quarters.

'Bloody officers bellyachin' for their

special orders,' one grumbled. 'You know –
pickles, sardines, turkeys, canned oysters.'

'Sure,' the other said. 'Reckon it's always
the way the minute a commandant's back's
turned.'

Lil ducked back into the women's privies.
It had been a close shave. One moment
later, and she would have been caught; the
alarm sounded.

Her second foray, timed when the sentries
slowly pacing the stockade catwalk were out
of sight, was successful. She reached the
shaft head in a breath-holding rush.
Instantly, she seized the handle of the windlass and turned as quickly as she could.

It was harder work than she'd expected,
but she was a strong girl. She brought all her
whipcord arm muscle to bear. With a creak
and a grating rumble, the gate lifted.

In the darkness beneath her, she heard a
trickle rapidly build to a·splashing torrent.
The head of stored water was bursting
under the rising gate, swirling and gurgling
on its way to the drainage channel under the
privies.

Her mind's eye gave her a picture of the
released water washing the privy muck up
against the obstructing sack of charcoal,
packing it into a tight dam as the weight

behind increased.

She crouched in the shadow of the low wall around the shaft head and prayed silently that the scheme would work, though she knew she couldn't trust wholly to luck; that she'd have to encourage a panic when the moment was right.

The rush of the escaping water didn't go unnoticed. A sentry on the catwalk called out to a comrade, 'Hey, Paddy! I hear water. What's goin' on down there?'

'Begob! I do believe some loon is a-hidin' by the sluice gate indeed. That or I be seein' a ghost!'

The word was out. Misfit Lil knew her hand was forced. She had to make her play – now.

She darted across the parade-ground toward the guardhouse. She was committed. Completely committed. She just hoped the sentries wouldn't go to firing their guns at her. But their duty was a routine chore during which they expected nothing untoward to happen. Judging by their frozen stances, they were utterly bewildered by her sudden appearance.

'It ain't no ghost. It's that damn gal, Misfit Lil!'

'Sure, I don't wonder if it is. Stop, missy!

Wha'd'ye think ye'll be doin'?'

And they didn't shoot her down.

Lil's spirits lifted when she also glimpsed that a huge, spreading puddle had formed outside the blocked and spilling privies. The dirty water was already flowing under the locked door to the commissary storehouse.

But she couldn't stop now to check on the progress of what she'd put in train, or its chances of success. Her objective point was the guardhouse, where she'd have to back up her risky ploy with convincing bluff.

She surged into the guardhouse, raising her voice shrilly, though only one sergeant was present on duty.

'Help! Help! A flood over to the commissary!'

The sergeant had been taking his ease on a cot. He jumped up, buttoning his tunic.

'Now what is all this? Why are you still–'

'I smelled wetted lime!' Lil rushed on, lying. 'I think it's about to catch fire – explode!'

The bemused sergeant, only half awake, staggered to the doorway and saw for himself that some of his night patrol had descended the ladders from the catwalk and were gathering excitedly around the commissary and the privies. The cause of the disturbance did look to be a huge puddle.

'Sweet Mary! You're right – something's up over there!'

His face white, the sergeant lumbered off to make his own investigation, thinking nothing of leaving his post in the hands of a nosy girl who made a habit of turning up in places unexpectedly. The priority was to save the stores in the commissary and, as young Miss Goodnight said, there was lime in there...

Misfit Lil didn't hesitate. The moment the sergeant's back turned, she skipped behind the high desk and took down the keys to the cells from the rack.

'Mr Farraday!' she called, as she hurried to the door of the solitary confinement cell. She got no response from behind the stout, iron-bound door but began trying keys with fumbling urgency.

'Jackson Farraday, it's me – Lilian Good-night!'

She heard a groan and dragging footfalls as the prisoner in the black hole mounted the steps up from the cold stone floor of the tiny, near-airless chamber.

'Good God! Is that really Misfit Lil?'

'Of course,' she hissed impatiently. 'Didn't I say so? Open, you damn door!'

'Well am I glad of that! One time I thought the Boorman's Wells posse might've shot you to doll rags in the canyonlands, Miss Lilian.'

'Tried to, but it didn't work. Skene, the disgusting swine, clapped me in his jail, promising all kinds of indecencies I had no stomach for. So I broke out.'

The lock's bolt shot back with an echoing clunk.

'Aah! That's the one... Quick, haul yourself outa there, Mr Farraday. We mightn't have much time to make a break for it.'

Jackson lurched through the door. He was haggard, and his unaccustomed eyes blinked in reflex to even the dim lamplight of the guardhouse. The cell behind him – the black hole – was undoubtedly very dark.

'Hell,' he said, 'I'm so stiff I can scarcely move.'

Lil was dismayed. 'But you have to move! Sheriff Skene is inciting a Silver Vein mob to lynch you, and Mike Covington – blast him – is fixing to hand you over. He believes you murdered Esther Boorman.'

Jackson heard her despair as well as the information. He said grimly, 'Then I guess I'll have to get myself together. I found out what Skene and Boorman are up to.

Covington wouldn't believe me either, but I reckon he'll have to when I lay hands on the evidence.'

Together, they struck out for the stables. Jackson staggered on his cramped legs.

The commissary had been opened up and men were milling about, packing bags of flour around the entrance to stop the entrance of more water. No one noticed the escapers till Lil lifted the heavy bar and swung open the stockade gates.

A shout went up from the soldiers.

But Lil was on horseback in a flash, and she and Jackson rode pell-mell out of the fort. A laugh was on her lips, whipped away by the night wind.

'Yeeehaw! It worked – this round for us!' she cried.

Jackson, being by age and nature less exuberant, didn't share her elation.

'They could come after us, Miss Lilian,' he shouted back in warning. 'And we ain't outa the woods yet.'

14

VOW TO KILL

When Jackson heard the whole of Misfit Lil's story, he told her the trick with the lime was a master-stroke but that she'd been a 'gutsy little fool'. He was filled with secret admiration for her pluck and resourcefulness. Plainly, she was intensely dedicated to something. The truth? Loyalty?

But loyalty to what? *Himself...?*

'It don't make any sense,' he said. 'Why did you get mixed up in what isn't your affair?'

'It is my affair,' she said tonelessly. 'I started the business when I got you in bad with the army.'

'Hmmm,' he mused. 'You got peculiar ways of deciding what's your business ... where it begins and more especially where it ends. Don't you think you'd best cut along home now to the Flying G – call on your pa's help?'

'You get my goat!' she snapped. 'I'm

throwing in with you to help find the contraband guns you've told me about. They're the
key to settling Boorman and Skene's hash
and finishing this rottenness, aren't they?'

Jackson said soberly, 'We might not find
the guns. The crooked law or the misguided
army might get to us first. I'm on the run.
They'd fill us with bullets. You'd be a fool to
cut yourself in on that. It makes no sense.'

She absorbed what he was telling her,
staring at him, letting the truth sink in.
Maybe something else.

Finally, she said, her voice shaky, 'Then I
want to make a fool of myself. I don't see
why I should leave you now. Because we're
both fools. You don't make any sense and
neither do I. We should get along very well
together.'

He shrugged, at a loss to understand her
moods and her reasoning, but he had to
make allowances, for she was nigh on twenty
years his junior and, despite her dress and
ways, a female, which in his book meant
naturally difficult.

'All right,' he said. 'No need to get touchy.'

Axel Boorman was informed by a whiskey
drummer calling in at his trading post that
Jackson Farraday – 'your wife's killer' – had

survived the death plunge in the canyonlands. He was being held by the army in the black hole at Fort Dennis and would in due course be brought to trial.

Boorman panicked. He'd no wish for a trial. He'd be called on to give evidence for sure. Farraday would obviously deny the crime. He was an educated man and could be a convincing cuss. He might guess the truth and accuse him.

Boorman had the ring with Jackson's 'J' on it, of course, but for some reason his accomplice, Sheriff Skene, had turned reluctant to present it.

As soon as the drummer rode out in the buggy he'd hired in Silver Vein, Boorman resolved to ride to town himself. The suspense was killing him. He had to know what was going on; to confer with Skene, his partner in crime.

Unknown to him, as he rode away from Boorman's Wells, Jackson Farraday and Misfit Lil were riding toward it.

Arriving hot, sweaty and bothered in town, Boorman stomped into the sheriffs office.

'Farraday's alive!' he jerked, pushing a cigar into his mouth with shaking fingers. 'What do we do about it?'

'Don't make no nevermind, Axel,' Skene

wheezed. 'The soldiers've got him locked down. They'll hand him over to me. It ain't no problem.'

'It is to me, Willard, an' we're partners, ain't we? You look to me for a better living. I cut you in, don't I? What trips you, trips me. I'll have to front up at the trial, show the ring–'

'Yuh don't show no ring, ol' friend. 'Sides, there ain't gonna be no trial.'

The impasse Boorman figured the exchange was heading for wasn't reached. He was chewing the end of his cigar nervously, reducing it to a squelchy brown ruin, when Skene's deputy loped in, agog with the latest news to hit town.

'Yuh won't believe it, Willard! Overnight, Jackson Farraday's gotten loose from the soldier-boys. They're blamin' Misfit Lil. The damned gal went straight off to the fort after she'd busted outa this jailhouse. She flooded the lime store, an' whiles they was cleanin' up the dangerous mess, she done broke Farraday clean out o' the black hole! The whole post's buzzin'.'

'Goddamnit!' Skene exploded, his face a mask of fury. 'That's the last straw!' He thumped his fist on his desk. 'The bastard's gotta be brung to book, fast. That li'l Goodnight baggage likewise.'

Boorman spat out the gobby mess from his mouth. 'How do we fix it, Willard?' he wailed.

'Axel, we're goin' to the fort. We gotta git the army in on this. They owe the community, I tell yuh. A homicidal crim'nal's on the prod here. An' this time he's gotta be shot down like a mad dog!'

The conspirators went out almost immediately, mounted their horses and put them into a brisk trot north to Fort Dennis. They reached its gates by mid-morning and the sergeant of the day guard conducted them personally into the presence of the acting commandant.

'An unexpected pleasure, gentlemen,' Lieutenant Covington said, rising behind Colonel Lexborough's massively impressive desk. 'Welcome to Fort Dennis. Please set yourselves down.'

He gestured to seats in front of the desk. Boorman flopped into one but the sheriff stayed on his feet.

'It's a scandal, Lieutenant!' he rasped curtly and without preamble. 'I demand yuh take action this day to recapture Jackson Farraday.'

A dull flush came to Covington's cheeks.

He felt guilt over Farraday's escape, but he'd not put in his years of training at West Point to be brow-beaten by the dubiously elected peace officer of a hick mining and ranching town in a ghastly stretch of frontier desolation.

'Mr Skene, it is not within my authority to mount a manhunt for a wanted man, even an accused murderer. The military is short-handed. I would be disinclined to assign men to the task without referring the matter to higher command. Moreover, there are other matters brought to my notice.'

'The hell yuh say!' Skene wheezed. 'What other matters?'

Covington realized he might have over-stepped the mark in his eagerness to squash the uppity sheriff. He'd only Farraday's word against Boorman and Skene and that, of course, was unreliable under the circumstances.

He backtracked. 'That is, to say, I've heard wild rumours, you understand, brought to me by Farraday and Miss Goodnight. I make no accusations my own self.'

'What are they sayin'?' Skene asked bluntly.

Covington coughed in embarrassment. 'I'm not inclined to repeat any of it. They alleged another party might have killed Mrs

Boorman; that a gunrunning operation had a local presence and was backing Angryfist's rebellion.'

Boorman paled visibly and sank lower in his chair. But Skene was ready to bluster his way out of the corner.

'Why, that's a heap o' horseshit! Never heard the like o' sich windies. D'yuh lissen to murderin' liars and fool kids, Lieutenant? D'yuh swaller shit?'

Covington squirmed. 'I'm not authorized to pass opinion, Mr Skene. The whole matter is outside my province.'

Skene clapped Boorman on the shoulder. 'Giddup, Axel. The man can't do nothin', he says. Waal, we will. We civilians gotta stop that killer an' his gal our ownselfs.'

'S-sure, Willard, another posse I guess. A bigger one. Call in the Silver Vein townsfolk this time, mebbe.'

'Yeah, sure, Axel.'

But outside, crossing the wide, flat paradeground on their way back to the guardhouse and the gates, Skene put Boorman right.

'I don't know how, but Farraday's on to us. We ain't goin' nowhere near Silver Vein yet. We're high-tailin' it to Boorman's Wells, lickety-spit! First thing we gotta do is destroy them boxes o' stolen repeatin' rifles, afore some nosy bastard hears what Farraday's bin sayin' an' believes it. Not ev'ry bluecoat is as stupid or trustin' as Covington.'

Boorman was in a blue funk. 'I don't like this one bit, Willard. Supposing Farraday goes to the Wells?'

'Waal, won't that be right handy? If he ain't showed, an' the guns are untouched, we'll wait, usin' 'em as bait. I'll bet he's a-hankerin' right now after findin' 'em, fer evidence ag'in' us.'

Boorman was unsatisfied. 'But what the hell do we do when he shows? *What if he's already there?*'

Skene coughed up phlegm and spat it out.

'Axel, yuh're an ignoramous. I vow we'll fill the bastard with lead, askin' no questions, is what. The damn interferin' gal likewise, if'n she's still with 'im.'

After his visitors had gone, Covington fretted as he paced his commander's office. Everything was falling apart for him – the failure to run down Angry-fist, the fiasco with the lime, the escape of Jackson Farraday, and now a confrontation with two prominent citizens.

At the bottom of it all was lanky Misfit Lil,

a young woman who hadn't the sense to realize that the place of a decent woman was in the home. His reputation was being reduced to tatters by her scandalous activities.

Skene and Boorman, it hit him, had treated him like he was the merest shavetail. On consideration, they'd been downright rude. Maybe he should have taken a firmer line. How exactly were they going to take matters into their own hands?

The startling thought also dawned on him that well, just possibly, there'd been a smidgen of truth in the outlandish litany of skulduggery Farraday and the girl had tried to foist on him.

Maybe, moreover, he'd spilled the beans somewhat by letting Skene and Boorman know the substance of the defence they'd put forward for their criminal actions. Could be he should have done something himself to check out the tales of contraband guns. If they were true, this was serious, army business.

Would he stand responsible for yet another unfortunate blunder?

His face darkened with a rush of blood and he went hot at the possibility, however remote. 'Damned if I do; damned if I don't.'

He smoothed his hair mechanically, put

on his hat and went to the door.

'Sergeant! Assign me ten good troopers. Send for my horse and see him saddled!'

15

SHOWDOWN AT THE WELLS

It was several hours after Axel Boorman had lit out in a hurry for Silver Vein that Misfit Lil led Jackson Farraday into the grove of cottonwoods close by the hamlet of Boorman's Wells where she had her hide.

In the deep shadows, they dismounted and Lil pointed out how good a vantage point it was for spying on all that went in the outpost.

'Mighty quiet over there,' Jackson said. 'The store looks locked up. Saloon, too.'

'The windows are shuttered,' Lil said. 'It's a sure sign Boorman's away. Shall we go looking for the contraband guns?'

Jackson frowned. 'We'll wait a bit, just to be sure, then yeah, we'll go looking. I've some ideas...'

'You mean you know where the stuff is?'

'Think so. Well, that is, I've got one damn good idea. Boorman ain't strong on imagination. He's also confident in his power around here, albeit that Esther managed to cheat on him right, left and centre. What he says, goes. He's landlord for most of the ramshackle holdings and holds liens over pretty much all of the tenants' stock whatever it might be.'

They waited and watched and Lil felt her impatience growing.

'I'm sure he must be away,' she said. 'Prob'ly gone into Silver Vein.'

In ten minutes, nothing happened. The nondescript buildings continued baking in the sun. Some fowl scratched in a yard and chased each other. An aged dog with three legs hopped down the main drag, scrambled into the shade of some steps and went to sleep.

'Right,' Jackson told her after an eternity that was actually more like ten minutes. 'Follow me.'

They quietly walked into Boorman's Wells and went furtively on to the empty front veranda of the trading post. The door was locked.

'Hell, we'll have to make some noise,' Jackson said.

A good feeling inside put a smile on Misfit Lil's lips. 'No we won't,' she said proudly. 'Picking that lock's child's play.'

'You purely never cease to surprise me,

young lady,' Jackson said softly. 'Go to it!'

She fashioned a pick from a piece of wire and moments later, they'd broken in.

'D'you feel like a burglar's apprentice?' she teased.

'Not yet,' he said, 'but I will when I've helped myself to one of these handy guns.'

From a rack behind the main counter, she watched him take a second-hand gunbelt. In the worn holsters nestled a pair of Colts – the Army model in .44 calibre. He loaded the chambers and partly filled the belt with cartridges from a full box.

'So now you reckon you fill the part, huh?' she said.

'In point of fact I don't, but I feel a whole lot safer.'

'What are we doing in here, anyhow?'

'I figger Boorman has the guns stashed in that storeroom he never lets anyone forage around in.' Jackson nodded to the locked door at the rear. 'Can you open that one?'

She took a look and was disappointed. 'I reckon not,' she confessed. 'It's some kind of fancy, patent thing...'

'No matter,' Jackson reassured her. The ghost of a wry grin flitted across his mouth. 'It kinda firms up what I suspect. Stand back.'

He took a short run and a flying leap at the door, right foot first. The sole and heel of his boot slammed into it. The frame split and the door crashed in.

Their rummage through the stacks of flour, salt pork, vinegar, whiskey and canned goods didn't take long. The long crates that held the rifles were back of everything else, but none too hard to expose. Farraday broke one open. He whistled.

'Winchester repeating rifles – the latest improved model in the catalogue!'

Lil said, 'Nobody will be able to ignore evidence like this. Boorman's fish is fried, I'd say.'

'I reckon you'd be right.'

But before they could savour the success of their search, the drumming of galloping hoofs reached their ears.

'Someone coming,' Lil said. 'Two, un-mistakably. Do we light a shuck?'

'Not a chance. The only way out is the way we came in, or through the living quarters. If they're headed for here, we'd be seen either way. We've got trouble.'

Lil's worry multiplied when the horses were reined in and the creak of leather and the thumps of feet on ground told her the two riders had dismounted. It seemed she and Jackson had made it this far and achieved their object only to meet with disaster.

They were trapped!

'No chance we can sneak away now,' she said.

'Stay still and silent,' Jackson hissed back. In an even lower growl he added, 'This ain't no place for a girl.'

Lil sighed inwardly. Despite the good account she'd given of herself in the canyon-lands and at Fort Dennis, he still hadn't accustomed himself to the fact she was as good as any fighting man he could ride the river with. Yet she knew when not to defy an order and kept her waspish tongue in check.

But playing possum wasn't going to work.

Outside, Boorman yelled, 'If you're in my place, Farraday, come on out with your mitts hoisted. I got the law here!'

Farraday jeered in response, 'Yeah ... I guess you might have. Sheriff Skene – the *crooked* law!'

'By God, yuh have gotten in there,' Skene wheezed. 'Waal, take your choice, mister, we got bullets, or a murder trial waitin' fer yuh.'

Lil cried furiously, 'Bullets or a lynch mob's hangrope, you mean!'

Boorman cursed. 'He's still got that goddamn gal with him.'

Jackson replied tauntingly, 'Kinda evens the odds, don't it?'

The whistle in Skene's windpipe was audible inside the trading post. 'No, it don't. She's jest a meddlin' li'l bitch! An' she's thrown away her chances fer good. This time yuh both die!'

'Who says?' Lil shouted. 'We got boxes of shells in here, and I can shoot better than either of you!'

No vocal reply came this time. The answer was the crash of a gun. The slug came straight through the open door and Lil felt the hot breath of it as it passed her ear. It hit a tin bath with almighty clatter that billowed echoingly and deafeningly within the trading post.

Jackson said, 'I hope you ain't hurt, Miss Lilian. Is that blood on your ear?'

Her head was ringing but she made out his words, and said not too obviously shakily, 'Don't think so. Think it was a close shave.'

'Too damned close for comfort,' Jackson said angrily.

He didn't have to tell her to hunt better cover fast. She found it behind the counter as hard on the heels of the first shot came three others. None had the spectacular effect of the first; they ploughed into softer store goods and the woodwork.

Jackson darted across the room and hunkered beside the door.

He waited till approaching shadows moved into his narrow view of the roadway. Soon as he spied the forms that made them, he thumbed the hammers of his newly possessed Colts and loosed lead.

Skene and Boorman saw his guns stab flame from the interior's shadows and leaped back, the storekeeper with a short screech which suggested he'd been hit and wounded, though probably only slightly.

The largely ineffective exchange of gunfire left a smell of powder and a tension in the air so palpable Lil reckoned it could be cut with a knife.

Covington's ten-man special patrol rode the trail to Boorman's Wells. The lieutenant had correctly figured that the trading post was where any showdown would take place. Where else would Farraday and Lilian Goodnight have gone to search for proof of their claims? Where else would Skene and Boorman go on their ruthless new manhunt?

'Sir!' an eager rookie with sharp ears

called out. 'I think I heard shots up ahead!'

'Aye, lad,' the sergeant said, then advised Covington, 'We're still five minutes' ride from the Wells. Could be we'll be too late...'

Covington shifted his hat and wiped the sweat from his brow.

'Jesus God!' he blasphemed uncharacteristically. 'Don't let me fall down on this one.'

He led his column into a thundering gallop.

The silence in Boorman's Wells dragged on. The sun kept blazing down. Flies buzzed drowsily over a heap of sticky empty bottles just inside the trading post entrance.

Jackson wet his lips and called, 'This is a standoff, Boorman. Your gun-running racket's finished. Clobbered. Backfired from hell to breakfast. You killed your wife your ownself. Ain't nobody gonna believe different now.'

'You dirty swine!' Boorman screamed. 'You were bedding Esther behind my back. You gave the slut a ring. It was in her bag–'

That was when Lil knew it was time to fill her lungs and yell her piece – the damning piece that Mike Covington had denied his chance to hear.

'The ring wasn't Jackson Farraday's – it was *Willard Skene's!*'

'The hell yuh say!' Skene broke in, his scratchy voice all cracking with anger. 'It had a "J" on it. "J" fer Jackson... Axel, yuh saw it plain!'

'Bullshit!' Lil cried. 'The "J" stood for Junior. I saw it when I was scarce more'n an unblemished rosebud and Skene was pestering me to go with him to his rooming-house in exchange for not telling my pa about something or other–'

'Shuddup, yuh crazy man-hater! Yuh lie, damn yuh!'

Lil ignored him, but not his protest. 'Listen, Axel Boorman. You savvy more than anyone how much better a liar Skene is than me. Don't you believe it? Skene's forgotten he offered me that ring if I did him what he called favours. He told me it was given him by his mother. She had the "J" engraved because Willard Skene was also his father's name, on account of which she always called him Junior.'

Boorman was getting her drift – and getting interested.

'Are you saying Skene gave Esther the ring?'

''Course he did! He was fornicating with

186

Esther every chance he got, long before Mr Farraday came on the scene. He was the one who really cuckolded you.'

'It's a lie, Axel!' Skene choked.

But Boorman was convinced. With a sudden roar of rage, he turned his six-shooter on his erstwhile sidekick and squeezed the trigger.

Lil, peeping over the counter, saw it happen. A raw red hole opened between Skene's eyes. He spun around, sending out from the wound a fine spray of blood and bone that hung momentarily like a halo as he fell to the dust beneath it.

'Judas priest!' Lil breathed. 'He's shot him stone dead, Mr Farraday!'

But Jackson was already moving like a big cat. Graceful but smooth and quiet, tensed in a gunman's crouch, he went through the door on to the veranda.

When Boorman saw the wiry frontiersman looming over him, he lost his nerve. Before he thought to swing his smoking gun and fire again, he hesitated. Lil observed his desperate, bloodshot eyes range around him, seeking escape on the wide, sunlit open roadway where there was none.

He knew the prowess of the man who faced him, and knew he'd done him grievous wrong. With a grunt of despair, he finally raised his weapon and hurled himself to one side.

Lil knew enough of gunfighting to know he was way too late. Two shots cracked and reverberated off the weathered sides of the buildings of Boorman's Wells. But the settlement's founding father never heard the last of the echoes.

The first shot struck him in the midriff. He fired his own the merest fraction of a second later, but because he was reeling it did no more than plough into the dirt between his feet and his trading post, raising a volcano-cloud of dust.

His revolver, released from nerveless fingers, thudded to the ground. He doubled up, hands holding his stomach tightly, as though seeking to stem the blood fountaining out. In his final moment, he screeched in terror like a dying pig. Then he wheeled and sprawled flat on his face.

Jackson went down the trading post steps and moved out to where the two bodies lay. They were both very dead, the blood darkening the dust beneath them.

Lil joined him.

'Well, you won't have to go up against either of 'em again this side of hell,' she said.

Then a bugle rang out brassily and a column of bluecoated riders appeared from behind the cottonwood clump.

'Hey, hey!' Misfit Lil said. 'The brass band's coming to town!'

The cavalry detail came charging into Boorman's Wells like it expected to find the place afire. At its head was Lieutenant Michael Covington, who hauled to a jingling halt beside Lil, Jackson and the corpses.

Lil rolled her eyes and groaned.

'You're too late, Mike!' She put a proud but bold hand on Jackson's shoulder. 'Jackson and I make a fine team. We've done all your work, and you'll find whatsoever evidence is needed back of the trading post... Still, y'all looked kinda dashing with your trumpet and things.'

Covington didn't rise to the bait for once. He gave her a look with daggers in it before turning his horse to the trading-post hitch rail and dismounting.

Jackson said confidentially, and in what she thought he intended to be a fatherly way, 'Don't be too hard on him, Miss Lilian.'

'Why ever not?'

'Because he means well, and he's an up-standing feller in the normal run of things. Someday, you know, he'll make a young lady a fine husband–'

It wasn't the time for such sentiments, Lil thought. Nor did she see herself as the marrying kind. If she were ever obliged to get hitched to the likes of a Mike Covington, she knew she'd cry all the way to the altar. The man she'd want would be mature and capable like ... but no, it wasn't worth dreaming about. Her inadequate years ruled it out.

Right now, she put a smile on her face, but tears of regret were in her heart.

This Large Print Book, for people
who cannot read normal print,
is published under the auspices of

THE ULVERSCROFT FOUNDATION